## A DEAD MAN

The first thing that caught Miss Bessie's gimlet eye as she came into the house was the bolt drawn back on the basement door. Just like the other day when they had all tried to tell her she must have forgotten to bolt it the night before. Well, she'd let them talk her into half-believing it then but not this time!

She flung it open, turned on the light—and screamed at the top of her lungs when she saw the man spread-eagled at the foot of the stairs.

She clung to the railing and went down a few steps for a closer look. White-haired man, blood on his face, eyes closed . . .

For all her strong character, Miss Bessie couldn't bring herself to go down any farther. She rushed back up the steps and began screaming again. "Help, help, there's a dead man in my basement—a dead man—dead—"

THE DAY MISS BESSIE LEWIS DISAPPEARED

## DORIS MILES DISNEY IS
## THE QUEEN OF SUSPENSE

# DORIS MILES DISNEY

## THE DAY MISS BESSIE LEWIS DISAPPEARED

**ZEBRA BOOKS**
**KENSINGTON PUBLISHING CORP.**

ZEBRA BOOKS

are published by

Kensington Publishing Corp.
475 Park Avenue South
New York, NY 10016

Second printing: August, 1988

Printed in the United States of America

*For my favorite legal beagles,*
*Judge Austin and Lawyer (Ret.) Maggie Hoyt.*

# 1

*Readers Forum, Kingston Dispatch,*
*March 24, 1971*

To the Editor:

The full impact of City Council's despotic edict, inflicting a system of one-way streets on Kingston citizens, was brought home to me today.

The fifty years that I have been driving a car I have followed the same route, up Cranston Street to Louise Street on my way downtown. This morning, however, I was pursued with blaring siren by one of City Council's gestapo minions.

He sirened me to the curb, goosestepped over to my car and wrote out a ticket charging me with driving the wrong way on a one-way street.

I tried to point out that from my own house on Cranston Street I had only three other houses to pass to reach Louise Street whereas I would have to go three blocks out of my way to conform to this new edict; that there was no traffic coming toward me at the time which made it perfectly safe; and also that a fifty-year habit of driving in whichever direction I pleased on Cranston Street was not easily broken.

But the gestapo minion paid no attention. No indeed. Taking his cue from his masters on City Council, he muttered something about the "grace period" being over and handed me the ticket which hails me into court next week on this ridiculous charge.

So another sacred liberty—the right to move freely on the streets of Kingston—has been lost. Not the first, not the last unless citizens take warning from this most recent act of tyranny and band together now in the never-ending battle against those who let power go to their heads.

BESSIE C. LEWIS
108 Cranston Street

# 2

Over a month before the day Miss Bessie Lewis disappeared her ex-husband, Henry Fletcher of Lennox, Pennsylvania, came down with a bad case of flu. He was convalescent in late March, at the time Miss Bessie wrote to the Kingston *Dispatch* but still allowing his landlady, Mrs. Ida Taine, the privilege of serving him breakfast in bed. Indeed, this privilege had been Mrs. Taine's for nearly a week now since Henry first succumbed to his illness. Not only breakfast but lunch and dinner were included in the regimen. Light meals the first two or three days but since then, building up Henry's strength, the trays had got heavier and heavier.

There were two flights of stairs to carry them up from Mrs. Taine's spacious quarters on the first floor to Henry's cramped third-floor apartment in what had once been an open attic. He had the cheapest and least desirable of the four apartments Mrs. Taine had carved out of her big Victorian house several years ago after her husband's death. Henry had found it cold in winter and hot in summer when he first moved into it but improvements such as an electric heater and window air conditioner had been added since at Mrs. Taine's expense.

In a word, she had set her cap for him.

Henry propped himself up higher in bed and called, "Come in, dear lady," as she set the tray down on a table panting from her climb and rapped on his door.

He was sixty-three years old, tall, heavily built, with a stately paunch. He had thick white hair, generally tousled, with a cowlick on top that stood up in salute and gave him a boyish look that brought out Mrs. Taine's thwarted maternal instinct. He had kept nearly all his teeth, somewhat yellowed from pipe smoking but still, all his own, a fine straight set that promised to last out his time.

His nose was a bit bulbous and webbed with minute red veins, his brown eyes popped slightly above their pouches, but he had a quick good-natured smile and easygoing expression that led people to think of him as a very attractive man.

Mrs. Taine was more extravagant; she thought of him as a handsome man.

He had shaved for her benefit that morning and put on clean pajamas. He smiled at her benevolently as she bustled about, a little sparrow of a woman with a sharp eye and tight mouth, fluffing his pillows and rearranging them so that they were less comfortable than they had been before, then setting the tray on his lap.

"Ah," Henry said in his deep melodious voice that might have brought him fame and fortune if he had ever turned to acting, "what an angel of mercy you are to me, Mrs. Taine."

But his heavy dark eyebrows drew together as he took inventory of the tray. Bacon undercooked, eggs overcooked, toast too brown—the coffee smelled good steaming in its pot but he knew from experience that it would be dishwater.

His landlady was no cook at all he had discovered over a year ago when she first invited him to dinner. That first time was a disappointment, since there was nothing he liked better than a good home-cooked meal. Presently, though, he decided that it was perhaps just as well that her table held no allure for him. It made it easier to turn down her invitations. Accepting many of them would have made it difficult not to repay her with invitations of his own and that, in turn, could have put him in an ambiguous position.

Until he got the flu he had kept his acceptances at a minimum. Now, of course, he was walking a tightrope; a sick helpless man dependent on her ministrations, putting himself under considerable obligation to her.

He knew perfectly well that she had marriage in mind. He gave her a wary, impersonal smile as she leaned over him to pour his coffee.

Why could she never cook even one decent meal, though? He sighed and poked a fork into his eggs hoping to find a little moistness left in the yolks.

There was none; like leather.

He chewed a mouthful, stirred sugar into his cup, sipped. Weak.

He sighed again.

Mrs. Taine laid the morning paper on his bedside table, chatting away about how much better he looked this morning, what a nice day it was, quite

11

warm, too, for March, would do you good, Mr. Fletcher, to sit by your front windows a little later if you feel up to it.

Henry said yes, Mrs. Taine, yes, I'm sure it would. Yes, I am feeling better. What a delicious breakfast, Mrs. Taine.

He picked up his paper. He hated being talked to first thing in the morning.

Mrs. Taine took the hint. "I'll be back in an hour," she said brightly from the door. "You get up and sit by the windows, Mr. Fletcher, and I'll make your bed up clean."

"Dear lady, it's too much to ask. You changed it day before yesterday. If it's just aired and freshened—"

"No, no, you'll feel more comfortable if it's changed." She withdrew, poked her sharp nose around the door. "Eat up every mouthful now, Mr. Fletcher. You've got to get your strength back. All those appointments coming up."

"Appointments?" He looked at her blankly.

"To show houses to clients, you said."

"Oh yes. Yes indeed."

He had forgotten mentioning a heavy schedule of evening appointments as an excuse for turning down her most recent dinner invitation. Truth was, the real estate market had been slow all winter with Fletcher and Stevens getting only crumbs of what little business was available.

Mrs. Taine closed his door and left. Henry ate as much as he could of his breakfast and flushed the rest down the toilet. In bathrobe and slippers he sat down by the two undersized windows in his living room with the paper. Before he finished reading it, however, he went through the ritual of filling and lighting his first pipe of the day.

It was an elaborate process that involved a pipe cleaner for the stem, a penknife to scrape the bowl, a hunt for his tobacco pouch, much tamping down of tobacco and finally the use of four or five matches and a good deal of puffing before it was drawing to suit him.

By the time all this was accomplished, bits of dottle and tobacco were scattered over the floor, the chair and his person and a small new hole had been burned in his bathrobe.

Mrs. Taine returned presently to change his bed and straighten up his apartment. She whisked about emptying his wastebasket, removing yesterday's papers, taking his other pair of pajamas downstairs to launder with the sheets stripped from his bed. (He had been embarrassed to have her find out that he had only two pairs of pajamas but she had shrugged it off with the remark that a man living alone didn't take proper care of himself.)

Henry had long since finished reading the paper but took refuge behind it again, watching her dourly. An estimable woman, making herself useful in his hour of need. A pity she had marriage in mind. A pity she wasn't a better cook. A pity she wasn't better looking and didn't have a nicer personality.

It was just as well she couldn't read his thoughts at the moment. He was resigned to her helpfulness but eying her as the sun caught multicolored highlights from her dyed black hair he told himself, not for the first time, that she would never get him to the altar.

That tight-lipped mouth of hers offered no giving-ness, no sharing of anything she had. Women like her, when they controlled the purse strings, could be pinchpenny mean in their treatment of a dependent husband. This he knew from personal experience.

He sucked on his dead pipe. Mrs. Taine winced inwardly at the gurgling noise it made. She deplored this untidy, this dangerous habit of Henry's—he might well burn himself and the house up some day, falling asleep while smoking. Once they were married, he would have to give it up. She would insist on it.

"Now, Mr. Fletcher, what kind of soup for lunch?" she inquired briskly when his apartment was in order. "Would you like chicken, pea, or vegetable?"

"Whatever you say, dear lady." Henry could put no enthusiasm into his voice. An article in the paper mentioning the increase in elderly welfare applicants in Lennox who could no longer get by on their Social Security checks due to inflation, had depressed him and the feeling still lingered.

Here he was, almost sixty-four himself, very little put away for his old age, no family to turn to—what lay ahead for him?

"You're in the dumps, Mr. Fletcher." Mrs. Taine fastened a shrewd eye on him. "No wonder, the bout of flu you had. You know what would do you a world of good?"

"What?"

"To get away somewhere for a couple of weeks, somewhere like Florida where you could soak up the sun."

"Florida? Getting late in the season for it."

14

"Not a bit, considering that it'll be another month before we get warm weather here. What about that cousin you spoke of a while back who bought a winter home there—couldn't you pay her a visit?"

"Why—" Henry looked at Mrs. Taine with a sudden brightening of expression. "Martha. She's only a second cousin, though . . ."

"Still, you did say she lost her husband last year. She might welcome company."

Henry quickly reviewed his current status with Martha Bartlett. He had only borrowed money from her once in the past three years and had paid it back eventually. He hadn't gone to her husband's funeral but he had written her a sympathy note explaining that he couldn't get away for it due to the pressure of business. He hadn't made any demands on her hospitality since his last trip to New York five or six years ago. She'd have no reason to feel he was imposing on her now if he wrote suggesting a visit. The more he thought about it, in fact, the more feasible it seemed. Just drop her a line, tell her about his flu and how much good a little Florida sunshine would do him.

He gave Mrs. Taine an approving smile. "You know, that might be an excellent suggestion you just made. Exactly what I need to pep me up."

Mrs. Taine, arms akimbo, head tilted to one side— if only she didn't remind him so much of a sharp-eyed little bird—nodded in satisfaction. "You just write to her now and I'll mail the letter later when I go out to do my shopping."

She was pleased with herself. She had no thought of triggering off anything; only of getting Henry away for a couple of weeks in the hope that absence

15

would make his heart grow fonder, propinquity not having had that effect.

There was also another factor involved. Mrs. Taine, truth to tell, was getting tired of playing Florence Nightingale with nothing to show for it, not so much as a tender glance from Henry to put on the profit side of the ledger. Here she was, sixty-six years old—although she had told him fifty-nine—up and down two flights of stairs waiting on him hand and foot; extra laundry, extra food to buy—she was careful with money—extra cooking for him, trays to carry up three times a day, prescriptions to be filled, other errands as well—it was all too much. Especially the past two days with her arthritis beginning to act up. If he had shown even the least sign of future intentions it would have been different, of course, an incentive, something to go on. But as it was . . .

Henry had a drink when she was safely out of the way, a straight shot. Not the time for it, only ten o'clock in the morning, but in his invalid state he needed it to help him get back on his feet. And indeed, after a second shot, new warmth and vitality seemed to pour into his sluggish limbs.

He went to his desk and penned a letter to his cousin in Boca Raton, Florida, telling her how sick he had been and that his doctor had suggested a week or two in the sun to speed his recovery. If a visit from him this time wouldn't inconvenience her, he would very much appreciate her letting him come.

Mrs. Taine sent the letter off airmail that afternoon. Martha Bartlett, sometimes lonely in her new surroundings and not yet adjusted to widowhood, replied with gratifying promptness saying he would be welcome whenever he felt equal to making the trip. She protected herself, however, from his tendency to sponge on what few relatives he had by adding, "If you'd like to stay on over Easter, Henry, that would be fine. The week after, though, I'll be closing up the place here and going to Nashville to visit my sister-in-law—I don't think you ever met her—and then heading north. Meanwhile, I'll look forward to your visit whenever you're ready to come."

The letter arrived the last Monday of March. Henry returned to work that day, making his way a little shakily from his car to the unimposing office he shared with Paul Stevens, a man many years his junior but with no more talent for making money than Henry had himself.

Fletcher and Stevens's only employee, who came in three mornings a week, was a stenographer, Mrs. Butler, who was helping to put her son through college by her part-time work.

Henry beamed a greeting. "Well now, Mrs. Butler, I hope there hasn't been too big a backlog piling up for me while I've been out."

Mrs. Butler lacked his Micawber touch. "Nothing much at all," she replied. "Few calls you've had, Mr. Stevens has handled. He's in if you want to see him."

"No one's with him now?"

Mrs. Butler shook her head. There had never, in her time, been a line of clients waiting at the door.

Henry left early that day. When he got back to his apartment and found his cousin's letter waiting for him his flagging spirits soared.

Who knew what Boca Raton might hold for him? Martha must have made new friends this winter, women friends, widows like herself.

Among them there could easily be a generous-hearted, attractive widow of substantial means. In her forties, preferably, with a little life and sparkle to her. And why not hope that she would be a good cook and homemaker, too, a woman who regarded it as her life work to make a man comfortable and happy?

By Wednesday of that week Henry was ready to leave, packing done with Mrs. Taine clucking over him, insisting on giving his shirts a bleaching to take away the dingy look that came from too many launderings in the bathroom sink. She could only cast a discouraged eye over the rest of his clothes. Those he had were well past their best days. He didn't seem to have even one good suit without pockets that sagged from having papers stuck in them or holes burned by that awful pipe of his.

Although Mrs. Taine didn't frame her thoughts that way, she felt that Henry's sartorial seediness gave him an aura of failure. He needed a woman to look after him, of course. Once they were married she would see to it that he spruced up. What point would there be in marrying him at all if she couldn't refer to my husband the realtor with pride in his appearance?

She hung over Henry on Wednesday morning while he carried down his luggage and stowed it in his 1969 Chevy II.

At eleven o'clock they said good-bye at the curb, Mrs. Taine admonishing him to take care of himself, not get overtired, not drive too fast, be sure to write.

"Indeed yes, dear lady, I'll write soon, I'll take good care of myself. Most grateful for all that you've done for me . . . Yes, dear lady . . ."

He got into his car and drove off, his rearview mirror giving him a last view of Mrs. Taine still waving as he went down the street out of sight.

He sighed with relief. Something better lay ahead for him. It had to.

There was no thought in his mind as he headed south of Miss Bessie Lewis who had divorced him thirty-five years ago and legally resumed her maiden name.

# 3

Henry thought of Miss Bessie, though, late that afternoon when he was on I-95 in Virginia and came to a sign that said KINGSTON NEXT 2 EXITS.

Kingston . . . What was it like now? He had never gone back. Had never wanted to.

Route 1 was on his left with the city just beyond it. He caught glimpses of it in the distance as he passed the two exits but nothing looked familiar. He hadn't come this way since the interstate highway was built or, for that matter, not for many years before that when Route 1 was still the main road.

Miss Bessie's house was in the old part of the city. Did she still live on Cranston Street — and still try to run everyone's business as she used to?

Of course. She wouldn't have changed. Just got worse, probably, with age. How old was she now? Good God, past seventy, nearly seven years his senior. She might even be dead, for all he knew. The last word he'd had of her was from a Kingston acquaintance he had run into in Philadelphia some fifteen years ago. She might very well be dead.

It gave Henry a sudden sinking feeling, this possibility. Crazy, senseless. What was she to him or he to her after their short turbulent marriage and all the years apart since? Nothing. Nothing at all.

Even so, he felt relief when he put the second Kingston exit behind him. No need for any more gloomy thoughts about Miss Bessie and his own mortality. She was probably hale and hearty still, the scourge of all who had dealings with her in the present or in the foreseeable future.

She had certainly been a scourge to him long before she revealed total ruthlessness at the end.

That screeching voice—couldn't he almost hear it yet?—that banty hen stance . . .

"I want you out of this house tonight, Henry Fletcher, and all your belongings with you. I want you out of Grandfather Pemberton's office by tomorrow night. And after that, I hope I never lay eyes on you again."

Well, she never had. Which was fine with him.

Oh, there had been bad moments at first but once the shock of it was over he had a feeling of freedom regained, of being his own man again. It was a delicious feeling. It had kept him from ever putting his head in the noose again.

Of course he had dallied here and there along the way, especially in his younger years, but whenever he found himself starting to get the least bit serious memories of Miss Bessie put him into instant flight.

On a practical level, he hadn't had much choice. He was never really able to support a wife and family. When he looked back on it now—which he tried not to do—he couldn't quite put his finger on why he hadn't been more of a financial success in the real estate business.

The depression was still going on at first but even when more prosperous days came along he hadn't done as well as he expected to. Except, of course, right after the war when housing was so short that a chicken coop would sell overnight. Even the money he made then somehow seemed to slip through his fingers.

Oh well, no use thinking about it now at the start of a vacation. Who could say what Florida held for him? A man's fortunes could change overnight.

Henry yawned presently and looked at his watch. Twenty-five miles south of Kingston, twilight coming on, it was time to think of finding a place to stay. He was still convalescent and shouldn't tire himself out trying to get below Richmond as he would have done if he had made an earlier start that morning. On the other hand—

Henry Fletcher's life story could be summed up in those four words. A Florida land development that foundered in a swamp, growth stocks that shrank into bankruptcy, a shopping center to be built in a pasture that was still the domain of cows. The list was as sad as it was long.

A sign came into view. HAYDON'S RUN EXIT 1 MILE, it said.

Around the next curve billboards appeared advertising motels at the exit: Howard Johnson's Motor Lodge and Restaurant, Holiday Inn, Haydon's Run Motel and Restaurant. In the distance, looming high on stilts, for all the world like men from Mars, were gas station signs of three or four major oil companies.

This would do, Henry thought, slowing down for the exit. Not the big chain motels, they would cost more than he planned to spend, but perhaps Haydon's Run Motel would offer more modest lodging.

But he shook his head when he saw it. As big or bigger than the others, swimming pool, dining room, expensive looking.

He drove past it in indecision and stopped for a traffic light at an intersecting road. A sprawling new Ford agency took up several hundred feet of highway at the intersection. A sign pointing to the secondary road on the right said HAYDON COURT HOUSE 1 MILE. In the field behind it a weathered billboard said BUCKLEY'S MOTOR COURT, TV AND SHOWERS. REASONABLE RATES. RESTAURANT ADJACENT.

Henry read this while he waited for the light to change. Wouldn't hurt to take a look. He blinked his directional signal for the turn and set off down the winding blacktop road to Haydon Court House.

He had forgotten, until he found himself surrounded by woods and fields, that off the main arteries of travel the Virginia countryside was still dotted with places like Haydon Court House, villages that were no more than wide places in the road and that had seen little change or growth since he had left the state nearly forty years ago.

A bridge spanning a creek had a sign that said, HAYDON'S RUN.

Some vague memory connected with the name flickered in and out of Henry's mind. He dismissed it as he came into Haydon Court House and stopped outside the general store for a look around.

23

A white frame Baptist church across the street; a secondhand car lot; a garage; two gas stations; houses thinning out down the road; the county courthouse dominating the scene, an old stone building with paint peeling off its pillars and a newer annex.

Just across the street was Buckley's Motor Court, a handful of rundown cabins with a small restaurant next door.

Henry pulled in at the cabin labeled Office and asked the elderly man inside if he could see one of them.

"Number Three's made up," the man said handing him the key, making no move to get up and escort Henry to it.

A double bed, a scarred bureau, a straight chair, an easy chair facing the TV, a bathroom with a rust-stained shower.

It looked fairly clean. Henry tested the bed. Mattress fairly comfortable.

He went back to the office. "How much?"

"Four dollars," said the man.

Henry paid, asked for ice.

"Ice?" The man looked as if he had never heard of it but after a moment of meditation said, "I'll see if the missus can spare some."

He vanished through a door that apparently led to his living quarters glancing back to say, "You go ahead. I'll bring it over."

A few minutes later he appeared at the cabin with a bowl of ice cubes.

Henry delayed the pleasure of a drink while he unpacked his pajamas and shaving kit, filled and lighted his pipe. At his age, a man had to think of his liver.

When his small chores were done he made himself a drink, a good jolt of rye on the rocks. He took measured sips when he first sat down with it, then told himself that he needed a quick bracer after all the driving he had done in his weakened condition. He tossed the rest of it down and fixed a refill, another good jolt that toned up tired muscles.

His third drink was milder. He took his time over it watching as much as he could see of the news through heavy snow on the TV.

He felt better. He felt fine, in fact, making his third drink last, brushing ash and tobacco off his paunch, letting the name Haydon's Run flicker through his mind again.

What did he associate with it?

He couldn't remember. Time for dinner.

The best thing he could say about the meal he had in the adjacent restaurant was that it cost only $1.75.

Back in his room, he fixed himself a nightcap and went to bed to sleep the sleep of good conscience and returning health.

He was ready to leave after seven o'clock breakfast the next morning and stopped at one of the village gas stations to have his tank filled. The sole attendant was a man Henry's age, a genial sort, very different from the motel owner.

"First customer this morning," he told Henry as he polished the windshield and outside mirror. "Bring me luck, I always say, if I get a customer soon as I open up for business."

"Been here long?"

"All my life, man and boy. Seen some changes

around here."

He couldn't mean Haydon Court House itself, drowsing in the early spring sunshine. "Oh, 95 and all," said Henry.

The man nodded giving the windshield another swipe. "Right lot of doings over at the interchange, them motels and all," he said. "Used to be, before 95 was built, nothing but backwoods around there, a farm or two, maybe, and the old Baptist church left to fall down of itself after they built the new one" — he pointed to the white frame building across the street — "thirty-five, forty years ago."

Henry looked at it. *Haydon's Run New Baptist Church* the sign out front said.

Some connection with Miss Bessie . . .

He drove back to the highway and picked up 95 South. As mile after mile of Virginia and North and South Carolina fell behind, the thought of Haydon's Run New Baptist Church came back now and then, a small puzzle waiting to be solved.

Henry solved it that night while getting ready for bed in a motel on 17 in Georgia, dredging up out of his memory the connection between the church and Miss Bessie. Some ancestor of hers had donated the land on which the original church had stood.

Over a second nightcap — to make him sleep — Henry was even able to recall the circumstances that had led to Miss Bessie's mention of it.

They were on their way to visit some friend of hers out in the country, taking a back road — the road that was now a busy highway off 95 — when Miss Bessie exclaimed, "Look at that, Henry, oh, just look at it!"

She shook her head over the condition the church

26

was in, a forlorn little building sitting in the middle of an overgrown field.

Some ancester of hers — grandfather, great-grandfather? — had given the land, it seemed, to the newly formed Baptist congregation of Haydon's Run to build their church on.

"Baptist?" Henry said.

Miss Bessie an Episcopalian, herself, explained that her ancestor had joined the Baptist church during some great sweep, revival or whatever it was called, that had taken place in Virginia during the 1840s. "The only one in the family who did," she said.

Something else had come up about the church later on, though, not connected with what Miss Bessie had told him.

Henry couldn't remember what it was.

Garters Guru supplied the answer a week later.

Not that Henry ever knew her name. Her brief impingement on his life came about on the only evening of his visit that he was left to his own devices. Instead of foraging in his cousin's refrigerator he got into his car and dawdled along the highway looking for a place to eat. The name of the town where he finally stopped didn't intrude itself on his attention since all of the Florida towns running together along the coast tended to look alike to him.

He found a place to park, that was the main thing, then strolled the busy street studying restaurants on the way. He stopped in front of one that listed the menu and not-too-extortionate prices in the front window to his left. The Delmonico steak suited his fancy and his purse. He went in, not even noticing the right-hand window which displayed a flamboyant picture of a young woman wearing pasties and a G-string hung with glittering garters. "Garters Guru, Florida's Sunshine Gal," the picture proclaimed.

Henry went in, made his way through a plethora of artificial jungle growth and was met near the bar by a hostess with a toothy smile who asked, "Would you care to sit out here, sir, or in the other room?"

Music came from the other room. Might as well get his money's worth . . .

He was seated at a table for two along the wall. He ordered the steak and had a martini while he waited for it to be served. A combo on a dais at the far end of the room played music that wasn't as hard on his ears as it might have been.

Service was slow. It was past nine o'clock by the time he finished eating and debated over a second cup of coffee whether or not to round off his meal with a cordial.

Suddenly the lights dimmed, the drums began a slow throbbing beat.

Henry stared. What was this?

A spotlight focused on a doorway beside the dais. Garters Guru made her entrance, red hair hanging over one eye, bright green sequined dress skintight to the knees, then flaring out in layers of chiffon.

She strutted and slithered, writhed and bumped back and forth in front of the platform singing nasally about something that Henry — was he losing his hearing? — couldn't catch a word of.

As she sang Garters Guru peeled off long green gloves, tossed them over her shoulder, unzipped her dress with a negligent air —

28

Henry gaped. Good God, a stripper. He had stumbled into a strip joint. How had that happened?

Garters Guru stepped out of the dress gracefully. Under it she wore the pasties and G-string shown in the window with miniature light bulbs strategically centered in them. The jeweled garters whirled around her thighs as she slithered through bumps and grinds moving in and out among the tables, stopping here to pat a bald head, there to chuck a double chin.

She came to a halt at Henry's table and before his hypnotized gaze dropped down on it, almost in his coffee cup, one leg dangling, the other raised revealing—well, he had no view of what was revealed but a burst of applause from across the room indicated that it won approval.

The next moment he froze with embarrassment as Garters Guru bent over him and sang insinuatingly, "You pay the mortgage, Daddy, you get the deed to me."

She slipped down from the table and moved on around the room bumping and grinding her way back to the dais. She turned slowly then to the pulsing beat of the combo, flicked on lights in pasties and G-string and advanced once more toward Henry, singing, "There'll be sunshine, Daddy, with me on your knee . . ."

Henry sprang to his feet, signaled for his check and fled.

At least the steak hadn't been too bad, he thought, heading back to Boca Raton. But that stripper! That song! Who'd want the deed to her?

Deed . . .

Suddenly, clear and sharp, brighter than the bulbs

in Garter's pasties and G-string, a memory from the distant past came back to him.

The year was 1931, he had been married only a few months and equally new to the real estate business, occupying Miss Bessie's late grandfather's law office—he first met her the luckless day he inquired about renting it—and on a rainy afternoon poking around through old deed boxes in the musty back room.

In one of them he had come upon a deed—or was it two?—relating to Haydon's Run Baptist Church. Yes, there were two, two grants of land given at different times. And papers of some sort—letters of thanks, perhaps?—mixed in with them.

But it wasn't Grandfather Pemberton who had given the land. Someone farther back, the one Miss Bessie had mentioned the day they went visiting downcountry shortly after their marriage.

And there was some sort of restriction in one of the deeds, wasn't there?

Henry tried to remember what it might have been but it eluded him.

# 4

Driving home at the end of his vacation, Henry spent Saturday night, his first night on the road, at the same motel in Georgia where he had stopped on his way down. His mood was very different, though, the hopes that had brightened his earlier stay not realized.

He had met an attractive widow at Martha's, yes, a woman under fifty, just the right age for him, very good company, suitable in every way except that she had no money to speak of, working as a secretary in Newark, New Jersey, and vacationing on a budget in Florida. A divorcée he had met later also suffered from the same insurmountable handicap of limited means.

And so he was on his way home with no better prospects than he had started out with; all he had to look forward to — if that term could be applied — was Mrs. Taine; and with her it was going to get more and more difficult to postpone a decision.

Henry needed several drinks to relax his nerves that night before he went to bed.

He carried relaxation to the point of almost falling

asleep in his chair when out of the blue it came back to him, the restriction in the deed that he had been trying in vain to remember. No beer, wine or other spirituous beverages were ever to be served on any part of the land or any building or appurtenance thereto given to Haydon's Run Baptist Church. In the event that this restriction was ever violated, the land would then revert to the grantor and his heirs and assigns forever.

Henry lit his pipe, got into bed, and settled back against the pillows to ponder this new recollection.

He felt it was accurate; which brought up the question of why Miss Bessie's ancestor had even thought of putting that kind of restriction in the deed. Had the old boy been afraid there might be drinking bouts on the church premises at some later time?

Hardly. But if Henry's memory of their being two deeds was correct, wasn't one of them for the church itself and the other, the gift of a much larger piece of land, intended for a future school, parish house, or something of the sort?

He seemed to recall some such explanation from Miss Bessie.

In that case, her ancestor had shown considerable foresight in the cause of teetotalism by the restriction he had put on future use of the land.

He must have been a fanatic about drinking; not the kind of company Henry cared to keep.

But what about the motels built on it now, all of them, no doubt, serving some form of spirituous beverages? How had they got around the restriction in the deed? Miss Bessie would have been on them like a hawk to point out that they were in violation of it and that the land therefore reverted to her.

Except that Miss Bessie, if memory served him right, hadn't ever known about the reversionary nature of her ancestor's bequest. Or where the original deed had eventually come to rest. Henry had meant to bring it up to her the day he came across it but she had been on her high horse about something or other when he got home that night and he had made no mention of it. Later it had slipped his mind.

Did she know about it now, though?

Who had held title to the land when I-95 was built? It must have skyrocketed in value at that time.

Puffing on his pipe Henry burned a hole in the blanket while he gave thought to the various implications that might be involved in the restrictive clause on the use of the land.

If his memory of it was correct, he reminded himself. If it was.

He would stop over in Haydon Court House tomorrow night and Monday search the title. It might be a perfectly clear one but if not, if it turned out that there was a bit of chicanery to cloud it, who knew what advantage Henry might gain from it? There was bound to be a lot of money mixed up in it somewhere.

He made good time driving north the next day, turning off 95 at the Haydon's Run Exit before six o'clock and again taking the road to Haydon Court House. This time, however, when he had registered at Buckley's Motor Court he drove back to the interchange to have dinner, settling on Haydon's Run

Motel whose name, he thought, best fitted tomorrow's research.

As he got out of his car in the parking lot he noticed a Kingston realtor's sign in the field next to it. ZONED FOR BUSINESS, the sign said. LONG TERM LEASES AVAILABLE. OWNER WILL BUILD TO SUIT TENANT.

For lease, not sale, Henry noted. That was interesting. But who was the owner?

He went inside. Ankle-deep carpet, subdued lights, a miniature waterfall trickling over ferns into a shallow pool; a poster on an easel announcing Historic Garden Week in Virginia April 24-April 30; a choice of two restaurants, the Rib Room, very plush as seen from the doorway, and the lesser Brookside Room.

Henry decided to splurge. He entered the Rib Room, ordered his usual rye on the rocks and sat back to study the menu with one eye on the right-hand side. Roast beef at $5.95 seemed to be the speciality of the house. Well, he'd have that.

His drink was set before him, his order taken. He picked up his glass. Was he drinking on the actual site of the old church or somewhere else on its tract of land?

Tomorrow should provide the answer. Even though he didn't know the name of Miss Bessie's ancestor, the grantor, the fact that Haydon's Run New Baptist Church was the grantee should be enough to give him a start with the county clerk.

So Henry thought. But when he put in an appearance at the courthouse the next morning the county clerk turned out to be a young man, new at his job.

34

His predecessor, Mr. Wilkins, who had retired last year would probably have been able to help, he explained politely, but as it was, he could only refer Henry to the Commissioner of Revenue in the annex next door.

"Commissioner keeps the land book, y'see," he said. "Brings all changes in deeds and wills up to date for tax purposes first of January every year."

The Commissioner of Revenue was a different cup of tea from the county clerk, a much older shrewd-faced man who nodded his bald head knowingly at the first mention of the Haydon's Run development and rolled down on the wall an area land map of the county. He then picked up a pointer and traced out the area Henry was interested in.

"Over a hundred acres, as I recall it," he said. "The Baptist church paid no taxes, of course, while they owned it but they sold it to a Richmond outfit quite a few years ago before 95 was ever built. Now if you'll wait just a minute, sir, we'll see what the land book has on it."

So it had been a direct sale by the church people to the Richmond outfit, Henry reflected while the land book was being produced. Miss Bessie had never entered the picture at all.

The land book listed the development company as Devco of Richmond, Joseph E. Krupusiak, president, and gave a Richmond address. The land was taxed as a tract of one hundred and two acres, more or less, forty-four acres of it still undeveloped. For tax purposes, the land and buildings already occupying it were assessed at forty per cent of their esti-

35

mated value.

Henry worked out figures with the commissioner and came to the conclusion that the land itself aside from buildings on it was now worth somewhere in the neighborhood of twenty-five thousand an acre.

The commissioner didn't dispute it. "Fair enough on the whole," he said. "Considerably less back seven or eight years ago when the first motel went up over there but it's been increasing by leaps and bounds ever since."

He shook his head. "Baptist church sure missed the boat on that one. Sold it for a song, they did, back in the early fifties before anyone—unless it was Devco"—he gave Henry a sly wink—"knew then where 95 was going to go." He paused to review his statement and added, "Mind you, I'm not saying those fellows in Richmond knew. They could have just bought it on speculation, figuring 95 was going to cut through that general area somewhere, and even if it was ten miles away, the value of their land would still go up enough in value to give them a good profit."

Henry nodded, keeping to himself his opinion that Devco had had inside information at the time on the proposed route of 95. It wouldn't be the first time it happened when a highway was being built.

He went back to the county clerk's office wondering if Devco had never sold any of the land because there was a flaw in their deed or if they just found it more profitable to lease rather than sell.

But there was still the question of how motels serving liquor could have been built on the land.

Even before they could serve it by the drink, they must have had beer and wine available for their patrons.

Had Devco taken it to court and somehow got the restriction lifted?

Henry searched his memory for a legal precedent in a realty case but all that came to mind was Girard College in Philadelphia which only white orphan boys could attend until a suit was brought and the court ruled against that restriction. What had happened to the case since? He couldn't remember but what did it matter when it was such an entirely different situation? He was only woolgathering until he found out just how the deed, conveying the land to the church in the 1840s, was worded.

But when he got back to the county clerk's office he ran into a blank wall. There were no records going back that far, the clerk said.

Henry's eyes bulged. "None at all?"

"Correct, sir," the young man said placidly. "Haydon County records were all removed to Richmond for safekeeping in 1861 after the war started and were all lost when the Yankees burned Richmond."

Henry, who had spent most of his life less than a hundred miles from Gettysburg and become, in consequence, something of a Civil War buff, couldn't let this statement pass unchallenged.

"The Yankees didn't burn Richmond, son," he explained in a kindly tone. "That's just a myth. General Grant didn't go near it! He was following Lee's army. The Confederates started the fire themselves when the government issued orders to blow up supplies before they abandoned the city. As a matter of fact, the first Union troops who entered Richmond helped put the fire out."

"Zatso?" The clerk's neutral expression said he didn't believe a word of it.

Henry sighed. Myths weren't that easy to kill. They had as many lives as a cat.

He returned to the business at hand and asked to see whatever records there were on the church's sale of the land.

"One moment, sir." The clerk disappeared into the files.

Henry waited. Was it going to turn out that the church's conveyance of the property was based on the doctrine of adverse possession — squatter's rights, so to speak, after a century or more of undisputed title to it? Might be that, he thought. Had to be something of the sort.

What it turned out to be was a special warranty deed given by trustees who were appointed by Haydon County Circuit Court. Henry then asked to see the chancery order book.

When he finally left the courthouse he was in a thoughtful mood, reviewing all that he had learned.

The church's board of trustees, acting with the approval of the congregation, had filed a petition with Haydon County Circuit Court to sell the land. When it was granted, Devco had then brought suit to clear its title of all objections and been given the special warranty deed.

Interesting situation. There were possibilities in it,

Henry thought.

His next call was at the parsonage of Haydon's Run New Baptist Church where he represented himself as an historian doing research on nineteenth-century Virginia churches.

"I'm afraid I can't be much help to you," the minister said seating Henry in his study. "The early records of the old church here were lost a long time ago."

He was ready, however, to summarize what he knew. The church was organized in the late 1840s, he said. A Mr. Sheffield of Kingston, who owned considerable land in Haydon County — at last Henry had the name of Miss Bessie's ancestor — and who had recently become a member of the Kingston Baptist Church, had made a grant of land to the new congregation on which they were to build a church of their own.

There were actually two separate grants of land, the minister added. The church, it seemed, had shown rapid growth at the start and the second grant of a much larger piece of land was apparently intended for a more substantial building in the future and possibly a school and parsonage as well.

The minister smiled wryly at this point. "The congregation's dream turned out to be beyond its reach, Mr. — uh — I'm afraid I didn't catch your name?"

"Fleming," said Henry.

"Oh yes. Well, as I was saying, growth soon came to an end. The war didn't help, of course. Haydon County had both armies fighting all over it most of the four years it lasted . . ."

The minister went on into details that were extraneous from Henry's point of view, although he tried to look interested and took a few notes.

After the old courthouse burned down around 1900, the minister said, and the present one was built two miles away from its former site which had been nearer the church, it began to decline in earnest. In the late 1920s, with young people moving away to greener pastures, the dwindling congregation abandoned the old church completely and built the one that was now in use, letting the other fall into ruin.

"So when this Richmond concern approached the congregation about twenty years ago and offered to buy the land at twenty-five dollars an acre, it seemed like a tremendous windfall," the minister continued, adding with another wry smile, "Apparently there was no thought of looking a gift horse in the mouth — proceedings were started immediately to clear the title to the land. The records —"

"Were lost, I understand, during the Civil War."

"Yes. When the Yankees burned Richmond."

This time Henry let the myth go unchallenged and instead prompted, "Surprising that the church had no records of its own to prove title to it."

"Well, according to the grandson of one of the original trustees — a very elderly gentleman now himself — the chairman of the board kept them all in his home. There was no full-time minister or parsonage in those days, you see. The chairman eventually became senile but remained jealous of his prerogatives and continued to keep the church records in his

40

possession until his death. No trace of them could then be found. He had no near relatives. Lived alone, it seems, with a colored woman taking care of him. She had no idea what had become of the records. So," the minister shrugged, "there was the congregation with nothing to prove ownership except possession of the land and obliged to go to court to obtain permission to sell it."

The minister paused, added reflectively, "Too bad it was granted so readily. The land, I've been told, is now worth at least twenty thousand an acre. The church cleared not much over two thousand on it when legal expenses were paid."

"That is too bad," Henry commiserated. "I suppose the money looked good at the time, though."

"Indeed it did. It built the Sunday school wing— with materials supplied at cost and volunteer labor."

The minister pointed out the window to a small one-story ell attached to the main building and added dryly, "It's named the Richard Goodwin wing in memory of the chairman of the original board of trustees."

"The one who lost the church records?"

"Yes, that was Mr. Goodwin. Chairman for over fifty years."

"Oh," said Henry finding nothing else to say. He got to his feet. "I mustn't take up any more of your time. You've been very helpful."

"Not at all, really, I'm afraid."

The minister walked to the door with him. Henry expressed his thanks and removed his portly self from the scene.

Very odd business, he thought as he drove off, and no mention whatsoever of Miss Bessie.

He headed for I-95. His next stop would be Kingston.

# 5

Henry had some difficulty orienting himself when he took the first exit off the interstate highway. No wonder, he thought, after nearly forty years. Then, following signs to the downtown area, a street name here, an old house there began to look familiar.

Hamilton Street caught his eye. Now what did he associate with it? Why, the ABC store, of course, that had opened in 1934, the year his marriage came to an end. It was a one-way street now. That was certainly new since his time.

He made a quick turn onto it, reminding himself that the bottle he had bought on his way north was almost gone and that he might need something to fortify his nerves before the day was over.

The ABC store still occupied its original site on the fringe of the business district. He parked opposite it, went in and bought a fifth of Imperial. His next stop was at a phone booth a block farther on. His nerves were suddenly very tight indeed as he turned the pages of the directory to look up Miss Bessie's number. If she wasn't listed it meant that she was dead — she would never have left Kingston — and the

43

end of the small seed of hope that had begun to put out green shoots, the green of money in his mind.

But there was her listing: *Bessie C. Lewis, 108 Cranston Street.*

He dropped a dime in the slot and dialed her number. If she answered herself—and he didn't doubt for a moment that he would instantly recognize that commanding voice—he would ask to speak to Mr. Lewis.

But the voice that said, "Lewis residence," was a soft Negro drawl—surely not the maid who had already been with Miss Bessie for years in his time?

"May I speak to Miss Bessie, please?" It was no problem to put miss before her name. He had never thought of or addressed her in any other way.

"She's not home now. She'll be back around five o'clock. You care to leave a message for her, sir?"

"No, thank you." Henry hung up, the first hurdle taken. Miss Bessie was not only still alive but active enough to be out somewhere until five o'clock. God, did she still drive herself too? Even all these years later it made him shudder to recall the narrow escapes they'd had with her at the wheel, governed by the firm conviction that she had the right of way at any time in any situation.

The most horrendous one of all was forever fixed in his memory; a dark rainy night heading home from somewhere in Richmond, Miss Bessie at the wheel suddenly deciding they had taken a wrong turn, swinging around in the middle of the road into the path of an oncoming bus . . .

"Jesus, Miss Bessie!" he yelled grabbing the wheel

from her, ramming the car up over the curb, missing the bus by inches, the driver swerving the other way, honking his horn wildly as he went past them.

"Watch your language, Henry Fletcher!"

"But you almost killed us, Miss Bessie."

"No such thing. It was all your fault. I had plenty of time to make a U-turn in front of that bus if you hadn't grabbed the wheel away from me."

She couldn't still be driving. She must have lost her license long ago.

Henry took the next street to his right, found himself coming out into a familiar, tree-lined square. Cranston Street ran off it at the far side, he remembered, but when he drove around the square to it he faced a sign that said WRONG WAY, DO NOT ENTER, and sighed in exasperation. It was hard enough trying to locate himself without having to cope with all these one-way streets. How long had Kingston had them?

He went back around the square to a street going in the right direction and after a few misses arrived at the one hundred block on Cranston Street.

He pulled over to the curb just past 108 and sat and looked at it. It was much the same, a tall-chimneyed brick house standing close to the street with a columned front porch and gracefully curved iron railing on either side of the steps.

A paved parking space to the left of the house as he faced it was new since his time. God in heaven, Miss Bessie still drove, it seemed.

Henry's gaze settled on the trellis that framed the side door. A climbing rose, coming into leaf, grew

45

over it—the same one as in his time? How long did roses live?

He had no idea. He thrust his hand between his belt and paunch and scratched. The belt, let out to the last hole, felt tight. He seemed to have gained a little weight in Florida on Martha's good cooking.

Another memory of the trellis stirred as he went on looking at it. Did Miss Bessie still keep a spare key there hidden in back on a nail?

They had been married a year before she ever told him where it was, and then only because he locked himself out of the house one night when she wasn't home.

"Don't you dare mention it to a soul," she warned him. "First thing you know, one person mentions it to another and then the whole town knows where I keep it."

She probably still kept it there. She was set in her ways even then when she was only in her early thirties.

As for Grandfather Pemberton's deed boxes, Henry felt sure they were still down in the old English basement kitchen where he had stacked them on a table himself when he cleared out the last of the old man's effects from his office and brought them home. The keys to the deed boxes were probably still in the table drawer where he had put them.

He had never known Miss Bessie to throw anything out. Especially not anything that had to do with Grandfather Pemberton, a model of perfection to whom she had constantly compared Henry, always to his disadvantage.

46

Bits of it came echoing back. "So efficient, so successful in everything he undertook . . . Always neat and well-groomed . . . Punctual, too, Henry . . . You could set your clock by him, coming home to his meals on time . . . Wonderful company, so bright, so witty . . ."

"Goddamn Grandfather Pemberton," Henry used to say under his breath.

His gaze shifted to the front of the house as he began to review with his mind's eye its spacious interior. There was the front hall, long and wide, with the living room and library, once Grandfather Pemberton's special preserve, to the right of it; from the side door a passageway led into the front hall opposite the library; to the right of the passageway was the dining room and next to it, the basement door with the steps going down under the main staircase; on the opposite side of the passageway was the kitchen, formerly the dining room and another small room, at one time a butler's pantry.

The basement, the focal point of Henry's interest, came under review next. The old brick-floored kitchen was to the left at the foot of the stairs. To the right was an open cellar with what had once been a maid's room and half-bath partitioned off from it.

The kitchen was a vast place, as he recalled it, running the full length of the house except for storage rooms across the front.

Two windows in the kitchen overlooked the garden in back of the house. There was also a door near them that opened on it. Against the far wall of the kitchen stood a monstrous old coal range; beside it was a long table on which he had stacked the deed boxes . . .

Henry was taken aback by a sudden pang of nostalgia that assailed him for a moment. What had brought it on? Certainly not any desire to relive the few years that he was married to Miss Bessie. For his youth, perhaps, the beckoning future, the hopes and dreams of a young man in his twenties.

He shrugged off the moment, scratched under his belt again and got out of the car. He might as well take a look now at the alley in back of the one hundred block of Cranston Street.

To reach it, he walked up to the corner where Cranston ran into Louise Street, turned left past the corner house and arrived at the entrance to the alley.

It was much as he remembered it; just wide enough for a car to drive into it, grass growing through a thin layer of gravel underfoot, evergreens screening the houses on his right, various shrubbery in back of the first three on his left, then Miss Bessie's tall boxwood hedge, too dense to see through until he came to the gate that gave access to her garden and slowed down to look into it. Rose beds, flower borders, statuary, shrubs coming into bloom, a brick walk through the middle from the gate to the back of the house and around to the side door, all seemed the same. A towering holly tree near the gate, though, must be twice as tall as when he had last seen it.

Another pang for lost youth, blighted hopes . . .

The alley ended at a high brick wall in back of a house on the next angle street off Cranston. You couldn't ask for a more private place, Henry reflected, as he returned to his car.

It was three o'clock by that time. He'd had no lunch. Might as well get something to eat and look for a place to stay. Plenty of time before Miss Bessie was due home.

He had a grilled ham and cheese sandwich, french fries, and a beer at a small restaurant downtown. He inquired about moderately priced motels in the area and received directions to the Kingston Motor Lodge just outside the business district.

He registered there and was given a room in the quietest section well back from the highway. He started to belch while he was unpacking. The french fries, he thought. They always made him gassy. Maybe a drink would settle his touchy stomach, a straight shot, taken as medicine without ice or water.

He felt better, his stomach quieted down, as he headed back to Miss Bessie's at four-thirty.

He found a parking place on Cranston Street almost opposite 108. There was no need for him to feel conspicuous with other cars parked all around him and a number of pedestrians, some of whom looked like tourists.

Henry lit his pipe and sat back to wait.

At quarter past five a green Plymouth with a dented fender made a wide swing around the corner from Louise Street, swept past him and turned in at 108, bumping over the curb. The car came to an abrupt stop at the side door, a short dumpy woman got out from behind the wheel. Miss Bessie, of course.

Her hair was gray now but still worn in an untidy

knot on top of her head. Her suit jacket hung open, the skirt hiked up in front.

She had never taken much interest in her appearance.

This was really the only thing he recognized about her, he thought, watching her step briskly over to the side door and go into the house. It wasn't just the gray hair. Rimless glasses were new since his time as were the dewlaps hanging down from her pudding face.

Who did she remind him of as she looked now? Someone . . . Not anyone he knew, though.

Queen Victoria in her old age. Yes, that was it.

She didn't remind him at all, not at first glance, anyway, of the Miss Bessie he had married. Well, how could she? Miss Bessie then had still had some of the freshness of youth left.

Now, if he had seen her away from her house, passed her on the street, perhaps, he doubted that he would have known who she was.

By the same token, she was just as unlikely to recognize him in any chance encounter. He had changed considerably himself from the lean young man she had married forty years ago. Which was, in this case, a good thing for him.

Lights came on in the house a little while later, first in the living room and then upstairs in one of the two front bedrooms, the room he had shared with her during their marriage—except when she was mad at him over something and he was sent into exile in a back room.

For instance, the night he drank too much at some

party . . .

"No indeed, Henry Fletcher, you don't share my bed tonight. I declare, the way I feel right now, you'll never share it again. You made a perfect fool of yourself tonight trying to do an Indian war dance and falling over the piano stool. I nearly died of embarrassment.

"No sheets on the back bed? Well, you know where to find them. Make it up yourself or do without."

That's settled. More lights came on at 108. Henry got out of the car and walked up and down to stretch his legs. It had become a tedious vigil with nothing to show for it so far.

At seven-thirty, slouched down behind the wheel trying not to think of how hungry he was, he heard the side door open and close across the street. A woman came around in front of the house and turned up toward Louise Street. She was wearing a white uniform of some sort. When she passed under the street light he saw that she had a medium brown complexion and black hair neatly arranged—not one of the Afros that in his opinion added nothing to anyone's appearance—and was probably close to forty years old.

Miss Bessie's maid, he thought, squinching down in an attempt to make his great frame invisible.

But the woman didn't even glance in his direction. She went around the corner out of sight.

He had no way of knowing that her name was Iris Lowe and that she was the daughter of Georgia, Miss Bessie's maid in his time; or that she worked for her five days a week from one o'clock until she had

51

served Miss Bessie's dinner sometime before seven.

All Henry knew was that she was another person in the house who would have to be reckoned with.

Unless luck was on his side tonight with Miss Bessie going out and giving him a clear field. If only she did, he would nip over to the side door, get hold of the spare key—if she still kept it on the trellis—let himself into the house, nip downstairs and grab the deed—if the deed boxes and keys were still where he had put them forty years ago—nip back upstairs and get out of the house with no one the wiser.

It all depended, of course, on Miss Bessie's going out tonight.

Which she showed no sign of doing as eight o'clock, then eight-thirty came and went. She was home for the night, it seemed.

At nine o'clock when the downstairs lights were turned off and her bedroom light came on and stayed on—bringing back the memory that even in his time when she was a much younger woman she had sometimes gone to bed early with a book—Henry gave up all thought of getting into the house that night. There was no telling how late she might read and no hope that she had lost the sharp hearing of her younger days in spite of having been subjected to her own ear-piercing voice all these years since.

He could at least check on the key, though, before he left.

For all his bulk, Henry moved quickly and quietly across the street into the shadow of the house, thankful for the small blessing that Miss Bessie's room was on the far side of it. He paused to look around and listen. No one in sight, no one at any window next door. Swift approach then to his objective, step mounted soundlessly, fingers slow and careful feeling for the key, blood drawn from one of them as it was raked by a thorn. But the key was there on the outside of the trellis, hanging from its nail. The right key, fitting easily into the lock.

Henry sucked his bleeding finger as he put the key back, made a fast retreat to his car and drove off in search of dinner.

At least he had established access to the house.

By ten-thirty he had eaten and was back at his motel asking for ice in the office, there being no sign of an ice machine on the premises. The woman at the desk filled a plastic container from somewhere out in back and handed him several folders with it.

"Perhaps you'd like to look at these, Mr. — ?"

"Fitch," replied Henry after a pause that lasted almost too long before he could recall the name he had used signing in.

"Oh yes. Well, Historic Garden Week in Virginia starts Saturday and next Monday is Kingston day. I'm sure you'll find the folders interesting."

"Thank you," said Henry without enthusiasm and stuffed them into an already bulging pocket.

But when he was settled with the first of four nightcaps he took them out, skimmed through them except for taking a closer look at those related to Historic Garden Week in Kingston, Monday, April 26. It would be a walking tour of six historic houses and gardens in the old section of the city, he learned, block tickets $5.00, single admissions $1.50, tickets

53

available at Historic Kingston Center, 278 Preston Street, or at any of the houses open for the tour. Luncheon, St. James Parish House, 147 Prince George Street, 11:30 A.M. to 2:30 P.M. $2.00.

Henry tossed the folders aside with a sour expression on his face over the memories they conjured up of Miss Bessie opening her house for the tour the second year of their marriage; everything turned upside down getting ready for it, Miss Bessie constantly bellowing orders to the extra help, Henry given no peace the day before it . . .

"Don't you dare smoke that dirty old pipe of yours in the house, Henry Fletcher. Think I want the whole place smelling of it tomorrow when the tourists come?"

Well, he not only hadn't smoked his pipe, he had stayed away until the whole thing was over. But then there was an uproar when Miss Bessie discovered that one of the tourists—at least they got the blame for it—had stolen some small object or other. Another offense, almost as great, was that someone had trampled down one of her flower beds—tulips or daffodils it must have been at that time of year—and Miss Bessie ended up vowing that never again would she open her house to the public no matter how worthy the cause.

Had she kept her word? Probably, being always firmly herself.

But her own experience hadn't stopped her the next year, the last year of their marriage, when the garden week tour took in a neighboring county, from jumping right into the middle of it, telling everyone what to do.

Miss Bessie wouldn't have changed since any more than her house had changed. That was why he felt fairly certain that nothing would have happened to the deed boxes.

Lulled by his fourth nightcap, he went peacefully to sleep on that thought.

# 6

By the middle of the next afternoon, however, Henry was thoroughly exasperated with Miss Bessie and, in fact, all the other residents of the one hundred block of Cranston Street who added to his surveillance problems by staying home most of the day, thereby making him, a stranger with Pennsylvania license plates, much too conspicuous as he drove or walked past 108 always finding his ex-wife's car parked beside the house.

He lengthened the interval between trips as the day wore on, worrying over how many old biddies there still were on the street like Mrs. What-was-her-name who had lived two doors away from 108 in his time and spent most of her waking hours glued to her front window keeping track of everything that went on outside. Mrs. What-was-her-name must be long since in her grave but no doubt had thrown the torch to a successor at her front window. There'd always been indomitable old ladies on Cranston Street, spinsters, widows, God-knew-what with nothing better to do than mind other people's business for them, particularly his, he recalled when he came there, a newcomer, an outsider. Miss Bessie herself had been one of them in spirit, thought not in age, even then, and it seemed unlikely that anything had altered much since.

Miss Bessie, still making things as difficult for him as she had in the past, obstinately stayed home all day, indoors in the morning, outdoors in the afternoon working in her garden. Henry saw her maid arrive at one o'clock and later caught glimpses of Miss Bessie out in back wearing some sort of outlandish get-up that included a ragged old sweater, a skirt sagging almost to her ankles and paint cap perched on her topknot. Once he even heard her voice as she yelled, "Iris, what's become of that new sprayer I bought last week?"

So much for the legend that Southern ladies had soft voices, Henry reflected, automatically quickening his step to escape the sound of that clarion call.

He moved his car around the next corner, sat and smoked his pipe, drove three blocks around to pass Miss Bessie's and note that her car was still in the driveway.

He gave up then, returned to his motel and didn't take up his watch again until after six o'clock. He parked below the house this time. Right after he turned off the motor the maid came out the side door, took the same route she had taken the night before, and vanished around the corner of Louise Street.

He looked at his watch. Ten minutes past six, well over an hour earlier than she had left last night. Did it mean Miss Bessie was going out to dinner and the maid didn't have to cook for her?

Yes, that was it, he discovered a little later. A car drove up to the house and Miss Bessie appeared, calling out a greeting to the two women in the car as she came down the front steps and a moment later drove off with them.

Henry walked past the house. An outside light was on and a light in the front hall, indicating that she wouldn't be home before dark. Out to dinner somewhere, he thought contentedly.

Half an hour later, with night settled on the scene, Henry strode up the brick walk to the side door at the firm pace of a man going about his lawful occasions. He rang the bell twice and then, sheltered from chance gaze by the trellis, felt around for the key, unlocked the door, restored the key to its nail and let himself into the house.

He stood for a moment just inside the door and looked and listened. Not a sound. Nothing to see but the light that shone into the passageway from the front hall. To his left, just as he remembered it, the kitchen, the door standing open; next to it—he glanced in—a lavatory new since his time. On his right the dining room with the basement door beyond.

He got out the flashlight he had taken from his car. The basement door was bolted, something else new since his time.

He slid the bolt back and descended the enclosed staircase, shining his light ahead of him, playing it over the two doors at the bottom, the one to the cellar on his right, to the old basement kitchen on his left.

He turned the light off as he crossed the threshold of the kitchen and saw that the two rear windows and

58

the glass panes in the outside door still reflected the lingering twilight in the garden. He groped his way to them around stacks of cartons and discarded furniture.

There was no sign of anyone in the alley or in the garden, enclosed on both sides as well as in back by the tall boxwood hedge. The door, he noticed, was bolted top and bottom. He slid the bolts back in case a hasty retreat became necessary and then drew all the shades.

That took care of everything, he thought, feeling snug and safe as he turned on the flashlight and looked around the room.

The old coal range, great black leviathan from the past, still stood against the far wall. Next to it, deep in its shadow, stood the long table Henry remembered with the glimmer of a white sheet covering something on it.

Henry hurried over to the table and whisked off the sheet.

"Well, well," he said on a note of deep satisfaction as he saw the black japanned deed boxes, lettered in faded gold, a dozen or more altogether, just where he had left them, unopened, probably, since he had put them there.

He stood for a moment contemplating his treasure before he pulled out the table drawer and began poking through the oddments it contained. He exclaimed again with satisfaction when he came upon a heavy old key ring pushed back into a corner, each key with a labeled cardboard disc identifying the box it belonged to.

He held the light close to look at the discs.

"Watkins Est.; B. Doran; A. Ramsay; Hood Est." None for Sheffield but one that said, "Misc."

Henry singled it out, the deed box that went with it, drew up a chair and sat down at one end of the table.

Copies of old wills, a fire insurance policy expired in 1927, an affadavit dated July 8, 1917, relating to a contested piece of property, an inventory of the assets of one Austin Wills who had gone bankrupt in 1925 . . .

Henry glanced through more of the same. Finally, a long envelope inscribed "Sheffield — Haydon's Run Baptist Church."

Pay dirt, he exulted, as he unwound the red string tied around it. Maybe, he admonished himself. Wait and see.

He drew out the papers folded together inside, heavy old paper brittle with age.

"County of Haydon, To Wit:" the first one began in ink faded to rust color but handwriting clear and legible. "This indenture made this twelfth (12th) day of April in the year of our Lord, one thousand eight hundred and forty-seven between Charles C. Sheffield on the one part and the duly elected Board of Trustees of Haydon's Run Baptist Church, acting for and in behalf of its congregation, to wit: Richard A. Goodwin, Martin L. Ormsby and Timothy B. Powell, the parties of the other part, in consideration of the sum of one dollar ($1.00) and of other good and sufficient considerations to him paid, has granted, bargained and given and by these presents does grant, bargain and give to the duly elected Board of Trustees of Haydon's Run Baptist Church, acting for and on behalf of its congregation . . ."

Henry skimmed. ". . . That piece or parcel ground in Haydon County bounded as follows: Beginning at the westwardly corner of Haydon's Run as laid down in the map of survey of Haydon County and running thence eastwardly two hundred and ninety (290) feet to a certain piece or parcel of ground owned by the said Charles C. Sheffield and known as line A-B in the survey . . ."

Henry skimmed on. ". . . for their use and behoof, their heirs, successors and assigns forever . . ."

He turned to the next page. No mention of spirituous beverages, no restrictions of any sort, Charles C. Sheffield unequivocally convenanting for himself and his heirs and assigns to forever warrant and defend the property hereby conveyed against the claims and demands of all persons whomsoever . . ."

Attached to the deed was a receipt made out to Charles C. Sheffield by the clerk of court for payment of the fee for recording the deed. Probably the reason it had been returned to him, Henry thought, rather than the church's board of trustees.

He glanced at the letter folded in with the deed. A resolution passed by the Board of Trustees on April 23, 1847, expressing the gratitude of the congregation of Haydon's Run Baptist Church to Sheffield for his generous gift of two acres of land and the sum of three hundred dollars toward the building of a church thereon. It was signed by Richard A. Goodwin, the chairman who, in his dotage, had lost the church records some forty-odd years later.

Henry turned to the second deed.

"County of Haydon, To Wit:" it began. "This

indenture made this seventeenth (17th) day of June in the year of our Lord, one thousand eight hundred and fifty-one . . ."

He ran his eye down the page. A much larger gift of land, one hundred acres, more or less, granted, bargained and given by Charles C. Sheffield to the same board of trustees of Haydon's Run Baptist Church, acting for and in behalf of the congregation, for the same consideration of one dollar and of other good and sufficient considerations . . .

But in this deed the clause Henry remembered. He read it slowly, carefully.

". . . The parties of the other part, by accepting this deed, covenant for themselves and their congregation, their heirs, successors and assigns forever, that no part or portion of the demised premises nor any structure erected thereon or appurtenance thereto shall ever be used for the purpose of the manufacture, sale, use, consumption, dispensation or storage of any spirituous beverage, liquor, beer, ale, wine or other alcoholic beverage or drink, fermented or distilled.

"This covenant shall attach to and run with the land hereby conveyed and be binding upon each and every owner and occupant of the same forever; and any breach thereof shall cause the premises to revert to the grantor, his heirs, devisees, executors or assigns and any breach thereof may be enjoined, abated or remedied by proceedings in law or in equity by any or either of such owners in reversion."

Well, there it was in detailed legalese, with receipt for payment of the recording fee attached, thought Henry, the deed with the restriction that by some extraordinary trick of memory had come back to him.

And there was Devco, for all its special warranty deed, building and leasing motels that were serving liquor in clear violation of the restriction.

Henry glanced at the accompanying letter extending another resolution of thanks to Charles Sheffield for his second generous gift of land to Haydon's Run Baptist Church. The second letter differed slightly from the earlier one in that it contained a postscript offering Chairman Goodwin's personal assurance that Charles Sheffield need never feel the slightest concern that his restriction applying to the sale of spirituous beverages in any building erected on the land would ever be violated.

Henry was beginning to feel a certain affection for Chairman Goodwin. If he hadn't lost the church records in his old age, there would have been nothing for Henry to investigate in the hope of providing financial security for his own declining years, coming closer and closer to him.

He put the first deed and letter that were of no value to him back in the envelope and restored it to the deed box. The other deed and letter went into his pocket. Tomorrow morning he would take them to a bank to be photostated and rent a safe deposit box in which to put the originals. No, on second thought, the bank might not let him run off copies himself. He would be better off going to the library where he could just drop a coin in whatever machine they had available and run no risk of other eyes profaning documents that might turn out to be his old age insurance.

Henry left everything as he had found it, keys back in the drawer, sheet spread over the deed boxes, shades raised halfway, outside door bolted top and bottom. He climbed the stairs and bolted the door that led to them. There was nothing then to betray his presence in the house. Or to keep him there any longer, he thought, as he headed for the side door—except for a sudden impulse that made him turn back.

He would just take a look in the library, scene of the final blowup with Miss Bessie.

He crossed the hall to it and halted in the doorway.

The room looked much the same. Faded old Oriental rugs on the floor, Chippendale desk between the two rear windows, solid wall of bookshelves facing him, fireplace to his right and drawn up near it, where it had stood in his time, Grandfather Pemberton's big leather armchair, sacred armchair with comfortable hollows in the back and seat then that his years of use had molded into it.

The leather looked black now, though, instead of maroon—or was it just that there wasn't enough light coming in from the hall?

Yes, that was it, Henry saw when he walked over to it and turned on his flashlight. It was still maroon, the same shade, it seemed, as the original leather.

The day he had burned it came back to him, a Sunday afternoon, he sitting in the chair smoking his pipe, reading the paper . . .

"Henry! Where are you, Henry Fletcher?" Miss Bessie screeching from upstairs.

"In the library, Miss Bessie."

"Well, come right up here and get this window

64

open. It's stuck."

He paused to knock his pipe out in the ash tray beside Grandfather Pemberton's chair before he hastened upstairs to do Miss Bessie's bidding.

If she hadn't rushed him with another screech he might have noticed a live coal from his pipe drop down between the seat cushion and the chair arm.

As it was, he hastened upstairs and got the window open for her. Then she had some other chore that took up a lot more of his time.

The first knowledge of disaster came from the maid yelling up the stairs, "Miss Bessie, Miss Bessie, yo' granddad's chair's on fyah!"

Henry had taken the stairs two at a time, run out into the kitchen for a pail of water and put the fire out in a matter of moments while Miss Bessie and Georgia — yes, that was the maid's name — had carried on together in the doorway.

Then came Miss Bessie's attack on him, heedless of Georgia, back in the kitchen, listening to every word of it.

"You're the most trifling, no-account man I ever met, Henry Fletcher. You're not worth the room you take up, you and your filthy pipe and your careless habits. Just look at Grandfather Pemberton's beautiful chair! He took such good care of it himself he'd turn over in his grave if he could see what you've down to it now.

"You're nothing but a parasite, Henry Fletcher, loafing around the house all day ruining the furniture. You haven't got enough gumption to earn a decent living for yourself to say nothing of supporting a wife . . ."

Henry couldn't get a word in edgewise as the tirade rolled over him. He never had been able to with Miss Bessie. And then, at the end, the words etched deep in his memory. "This is the last straw, Henry Fletcher. You start packing right this minute. I want you out of this house tonight and all your belongings with you. I want you out of Grandfather Pemberton's office by tomorrow night. No later than that, hear? And after that I hope I never lay eyes on you again."

Well, it had taken him a little longer than that to clear out the office, wind up his affairs in Kingston. Within the week, though, he had checked out of the hotel and was on his way back to Lennox, thankful to say what good-bys had to be said and leave the gossip and curious stares behind him.

Miss Bessie, being a law unto herself, had just faced it all down. He could think of nothing, in fact, with the possible exception of an atom bomb, that Miss Bessie wouldn't be able to face down. She made no bones about telling people that she was done with him, had put him out of her house and would, in due course, get a divorce from him . . .

Time to leave, Henry thought, turning away from the scene of his downfall. No use pushing his luck too far, no guarantee of how long it would be before Miss Bessie's return.

But as he left, his departure as discreet as his arrival, the pleasing thought came that he might be one up on her at last; that she would never have the chance now to bring a suit over her ancestor's — was it great-grandfather or great-great? — land.

God knew she had been quick enough to sue in the past over any infringement, real or fancied, of her rights. He himself could recall two suits begun during their marriage — one against a tenant of one of her houses over some sort of damage to it, the other over some disputed land boundary.

It added an extra fillip to Henry's hopes that if he could make any money out of the deed, he would be getting his own back at Miss Bessie. The only pity was, he could never let her know about it.

# 7

What name should he use with Devco? Henry weighed the matter as he came out of the Kingston National Bank, Plaza Branch, at eleven o'clock the next morning, pausing outside to put one of the keys to the safe deposit box he had just rented in one pocket and the second key in another.

Some variant of his own name? Henry . . . Patrick Henry came to mind. What could be more appropriate here in Virginia? All right, he thought, as he walked along the arcade to a pay station. Patrick. Patrick who?

As he was getting out change to make his phone call, the legend of Robin Hood, robbing the rich to give money to the poor, occurred to him. It might well be considered a parallel to his own situation, Devco the rich corporation, he the poor man, only seeking a little financial ease apart from, God forbid, Mrs. Taine.

Robin Hood. Henry chuckled over the conceit while he dialed information to ask for Devco's number. Should he be Patrick Robin or Patrick Hood? Better be Hood. Robin had a made-up sound, didn't it? On the other hand, though, Hood had unpleasant connotations, that he wouldn't care to associate with himself.

Well, then, make it Patrick Robin.

He jotted down Devco's number, hung up and consulted his notebook for another look at the name of the president of the company, taken from the Commissioner of Revenue's land book. Joseph Krupusiak. Polish, wasn't it? Took a little pronouncing.

Henry fished the dime information had returned out of the slot, dialed the operator, got his dime back again and put in the twenty-five cents she asked for.

"Devco," said a bright young voice a moment later.

"Mr. Krupu-siak," Henry said stumbling over the name.

"One moment, please."

A buzzing sound was followed by another bright young voice saying, "Mr. Krupusiak's office," the name tripping smoothly off the young woman's tongue.

Well, she had practice saying it, of course. As Henry might have himself before this business was over.

"May I speak to Mr. Krupusiak, please?"

"Oh, I'm sorry, he's in conference right now."

Standard runaround, thought Henry.

"This is Mr. Krupusiak's secretary," the voice continued. "Is there any message, sir? If you'll give me your name — ?"

"Patrick Robin. How soon can I reach Mr. Krupusiak? If you'll just tell him I called and that I'd like to talk to him about the Haydon's Run development."

"Oh, if it's the land leases, they're handled by — "

69

"No, it's not that." Henry spoke firmly. "There's a certain complication connected with the title to the land that I'd prefer to talk over with Mr. Krupus-iak himself."

"Well . . . if you'll call back in half an hour or leave a number where he can reach you—"

"Thank you, I'll call back." Henry hung up before the young woman could press him further. But at least he had said enough, he thought, to get Krupusiak in person next time around.

In the meantime, might as well go back to the motel. There was a pay phone near it where he could make his next call and have a drink in his room first. Not that he approved of drinking before noon, but it seemed permissible under the circumstances with his stomach rumbling a bit, giving him a peckish feeling. A drink might help to quiet it down.

This time he was put through to his man without delay. The secretary said, "Oh yes, Mr. Robin." Then a curt voice came on saying, "Krupusiak."

Henry made a cautious approach, mindful of the secretary who might be listening in. "It just happens, Mr. Krupusiak, that the original deed to the land you bought from Haydon's Run Baptist Church has come into my possession. It has a restrictive clause in it that might be of some interest to you."

"Don't know why," Krupusiak replied curt as ever. "Took the case to court, got the title cleared—"

"I understand you took it to court because there was no record of title to it," Henry interrupted trying to match his curtness. "But now the original deed has turned up and, as I said, it does have this restrictive clause that could lead to complications. It might be to your advantage to talk it over with me, Mr. Krupusiak." The name was coming more easily now.

Silence at the other end. Then Krupusiak asked, "You here in Richmond now?"

"No, nor do I expect to be. But how about meeting at the Haydon's Run Motel? That seems a good choice seeing that our business is connected with it."

"Suits me," said Krupusiak, reflecting that it would be easy to keep track of comings and goings there. "Let's make it the cocktail lounge around eight-thirty tonight. How'll I know you?"

"I'm six feet tall, white hair, brown plaid jacket. I'll try to get a table for two. You'll recognize me all right."

"Okay." Krupusiak hung up, Henry following suit a moment later, feeling pleased with himself.

He would go back to his room now and have another drink to celebrate, so to speak, a good start on the matter at hand.

Krupusiak had different feelings. He told his secretary to hold any calls, lit a cigar from the box on his desk and crossed the deep-piled carpet of his office, a corner room with banks of windows on the two outside walls. He paid no attention to the view that offered a sweeping panorama of downtown Richmond from the soaring glass and concrete of new office buildings to mellow old nineteenth-century brick edifices of every sort; from a distant glimpse of the James River to the historic state capitol and the spire of St. Paul's.

He stood puffing on his cigar, a short stocky figure, broad-shouldered, powerful looking, with a close-cropped bullet head, rough-hewn face that could assume a hearty surface geniality and ice-cold eyes.

He had a highly developed instinct for trouble — he wouldn't have got where he was without it — and Patrick Robin's call, instinct said, conveyed a strong whiff of it. Original deed, restrictive clause, for chrissake. After all his lawyers had done, too, getting him a clear title to the land.

Should he call them now, get Sam Peters, maybe, to go up to Haydon's Run with him tonight?

No, he decided, puffing harder on his cigar, letting the ash fall unheeded to the carpet. No, not until he had some idea what this Patrick Robin was up to. It smelled like blackmail to him. If it was, if Robin was out to feather his nest at Krupusiak's expense — he grinned tightly at his play on words — he'd soon find out, by God, that he'd picked the wrong customer for it.

Joe Krupusiak, a mixture of German, Welsh, Czech blood, had come up the hard way from dirt-poor beginnings in a West Virginia coal mining town. His education, such as was available in a one-room schoolhouse, had ended at the age of fourteen. He had got what he could out of it; he was bright and ambitious, driven by the determination to find a better life for himself than following his father into the mines.

He left home in the middle of the depression and ended up in Richmond working for a builder at starvation wages but learning his trade on the job and, above all, learning to bulldoze his way through anyone or anything that stood in his way.

Devco was his creation. Where he got the capital to

finance and expand it would not bear examination; ruthlessness and hard work did the rest.

Krupusiak had married late, only nine years ago, above his station, a Richmond girl with no money but good education and family background. He was forty-one at the time, she twenty-seven. He had bought back her ancestral home, long gone out of the family, spent a small fortune remodeling it, restoring a garden that had once been famous and was on its way to becoming famous again. There were two children now, a boy and a girl.

His marriage, by and large, was a good investment, he thought. It had given him a thin veneer of polish he had lacked before. It had opened doors to him, led to lucrative contacts as his wife's husband that would have been totally out of reach to him on his own.

So he had prospered. And what he had he meant to keep. To increase.

This was the man who was expected to provide Henry Fletcher's nest egg.

Presently Krupusiak went back to his desk and dialed a number on his private phone.

It was answered on the second ring.

"Breck?" He clamped his cigar in the corner of his mouth and talked around it. "Got a job for you and Elwood tonight at Haydon's Run Motel. I'm meeting a guy there at eight-thirty, six feet tall, white hair, wearing a brown plaid jacket. I want you and Elwood there by seven o'clock. Have Elwood stay outside to check on his car and see if he brings anyone with him. You wait in the lobby, Breck, and keep an eye on what goes on, whether this guy registers there, meets anyone or anything at all. Got that?"

"Sure, Mr. K."

"I'm meetıng the guy in the cocktail lounge. Once we've met, you and Elwood sit in back where he won't notice you. If I want to make contact to give you further instructions, I'll go to the men's room. You wait a minute or two and then follow me in."

Krupusiak paused. "Got it all straight now?"

"Right, Mr. K. No sweat."

"Make sure you fill your gas tank in case I want you to tail him."

"Will do."

"Okay then." Krupusiak hung up, not troubling himself with the small courtesy of saying good-by.

He saw no need for courtesy in dealing with them, engaging in the sort of banter that he might take the time for in contacts with his regular construction crews. Breck and Elwood, although they appeared on the payroll as security guards, watchmen at various development sites, fell into a different category. They were Krupusiak's strong-arm men, occasionally called upon for extracurricular duties. Sometimes they took along the guns that they were not supposed to carry when they were away from their security jobs but mostly they relied on their fists. They were big men both, brutal in carrying out orders, ready to beat up, even to the point of putting in the hospital, anyone who gave Krupusiak trouble, the only restraint being that the assault must never be traced back to him.

Breck had once been a deputy sheriff in West Virginia but had lost his badge for manhandling a suspect who turned out to be the wrong person.

Elwood had once been a prison guard but had

found it expedient to resign at the start of an investigation on the abuse of prisoners.

Krupusiak paid them cash bonuses for extra services. He commanded their respect, loyalty, unquestioning obedience. Also, a dividend money could not have bought, fear of him. They sensed that he was, in some ways, more brutal than they were themselves.

He was vastly smarter too. Which didn't mean much, considering the combined mentalities of Breck and Elwood. They were a stupid pair.

That would be Henry Fletcher's only advantage over them.

# 8

Henry had decided to ask Krupusiak for two hundred and fifty thousand dollars. It sounded like less money, he thought, than a quarter of a million.

He had no trouble arriving at this figure. One hundred acres valued at twenty-five thousand an acre came to two and a half million. What he would ask for represented a straight ten percent, a bit more than most realty fees, it was true, but no more than an agent's fee in other fields of activity.

The original two-acre grant, with no restrictions put on its use, did not come into the picture; would not have, in any case, Henry's study of the land map had indicated, since it seemed that a gas station now occupied that piece of land.

Henry didn't really hope to get as much as he asked for, of course; it just gave him room to bargain. But he wouldn't take less than two hundred thousand, he told himself.

Or would he? Even half that much . . .

Wait and see.

At ten minutes past eight that night he turned in at the parking lot of the Haydon's Run Motel. Although it was a Wednesday night with the lot not nearly filled, Henry didn't notice the big moon-faced man sitting in a blue Pontiac Firebird parked near the entrance. Vaguely, however, he noticed a sticker on the rear bumper that said *America Love It or Leave It,* and tried for a moment to remember what someone he knew had said about its arrogant message; something to the effect that it would be more honest if it read America Love It My Way or Leave It.

Elwood took careful notice of him, six feet tall, white hair, brown plaid jacket, the guy Mr. K. was coming to meet.

As soon as Henry went inside Elwood got out of the Firebird and strolled past Henry's car to write down the make, color, and Pennsylvania license number. Then he followed him inside to make sure Breck hadn't missed him.

Henry, all unaware, crossed the lobby to the cocktail lounge, no more than an ell off the Rib Room, all that would have been needed, he thought, before liquor-by-the-drink became legal in Virginia.

There was a table free by the windows. He sat down at it and looked around. Two or three groups at other tables, only one man alone, a big, lantern-jawed man in a far corner who met Henry's questioning look with a blank stare. Not Krupusiak.

It was Breck. By the time Elwood joined him, the waiter had diverted Henry's attention. He ordered his usual rye on the rocks.

Just as the waiter served it, a man came into the room, short, stocky, well-dressed, pausing in the doorway for an unhurried survey of those present.

Krupusiak, Henry thought, even before the other spotted him and headed toward his table.

"Mr. Robin?"

"Yes." Henry stood up, started to hold out his hand, drew it back, unsure of the etiquette the occasion demanded.

Krupusiak ignored the gesture. He pulled out a chair, beckoning the waiter and ordered bourbon and water. "Old Granddad," he added. "And a separate check."

He said nothing then until his drink was served. He took a swallow of it, cold eyes fixed on Henry over the rim of his glass.

"Well, what about the title?" he asked abruptly.

Henry couldn't resist a touch of drama. "This," he said, pointing to his glass. "Alcoholic beverage sold on the premises."

"So?"

"Never to be manufactured, sold or otherwise dispensed on the land given to Haydon's Run Baptist Church or in any building ever erected on it. That's the restriction in the deed, Mr. Krupusiak; and if there's a violation of it, the land reverts to the heirs or assigns of the grantor."

Henry paused, assumed a pensive expression and shook his head. "Too bad you didn't know about the restriction, Mr. Krupusiak; it would have made you stop and think twice about the enormous amount of money you'd have to put into a development like this, wouldn't it? As it stands now, it presents quite a problem for you. Just the leases, for example. They warrant quiet and peaceful possession of the premises

78

as long as the lessees pay their rent, don't they?" Another headshake. "Think of the suits the lessees could bring against you, Mr. Krupusiak. To say nothing of the heirs of the grantor taking you to court for restoration of their lawful property now that—"

"Bullshit," said Krupusiak. "I don't know what you're up to but I've been to court already and I got clear title to the land."

"Not quite. Special warranty deed."

"Which is clear title. My lawyers saw to that, went through the whole works. Petitioned the county circuit court in the church's name to give them the right to sell me the land, got a decree against possible heirs of the original grantor, decree of the court clearing my title of all objections."

"True. On the other hand, I have photostats here of the original deed and the letter of thanks from the board of trustees to the grantor—" Henry reached into his pocket and brought out the photostats.

He ordered another drink while Krupusiak studied them and sipped it slowly, his gaze on the bullet head opposite him bent over the documents.

It took some time. Krupusiak was a slow reader, it seemed, or else stalling while he tried to think of a way out.

But there was no lessening of his assurance when he finally raised his head and favored Henry with another long hard stare—gray eyes like frozen water, belying the genial smile he gave the waiter when he signaled him for another drink.

He slid the photostats back across the table with a

79

contemptuous flick of the hand. "Never stand up in court. Not in a million years."

"Maybe not." Henry paused for effect after this concession and then added gently, "But it wouldn't do you much good, either, Mr. Krupusiak, if you had to fight it. Happens I know who the heirs are and that they're the type to sue at the drop of a hat. Even if you have title insurance, it's only for the few thousands you paid for the land, isn't it? A drop in the bucket, let's say. Meanwhile, could you lease or build on the rest of it while it was in litigation? I doubt you could, Mr. Krupusiak, with a cloud on its title. It could drag on for years too . . ."

The waiter brought Krupusiak's drink. He drank, drummed on the table with thick strong fingers — strong enough to choke Henry to death — and considered his position. He couldn't even consider a lawsuit over his title to the land, the rents tied up in escrow, new tenants shying away — God, what a mess it would be.

What was the answer then? He had never in his life stood still for any kind of shakedown and he wasn't about to start now. He'd kill that blackmailing bastard across the table first.

He lowered his gaze to his glass for fear that Henry could read his thoughts.

With a great effort Krupusiak controlled the fury boiling up in him and said on a judicious note, "I doubt that any good lawyer would take a case like this on behalf of Sheffield's heirs. He'd know it was a loser. He'd advise the heirs against it."

"Would he? I don't know about that, Mr. Krupusiak. It's a tricky situation, I'll grant, but it's got possibilities. No precedents, at least none I've ever heard of. He'd be in uncharted waters, I should think, but so would the court. Tricky. You never know how it might turn out." Henry's bulging brown eyes had an earnest look. "I wouldn't want to place any bets on it myself, either way."

Neither would Krupusiak, he acknowledged to himself inwardly. There was the goddamn deed with that restriction put in by the goddamn pussyfooting temperance nut, Charles Sheffield, expressing a clear intent . . .

Krupusiak brooded cupping his glass in both hands. Pride was one thing, like never having stood still for a shakedown in his life, but common sense was another. If this bastard, this cheap trickster — his glance swept over Henry's unprepossessing clothes, his slightly seedy look, the aura of failure they and his whole approach conveyed — could be bought off for a few thousand bucks, wasn't it plain common sense to take that way out?

"Just to save trouble," he said, "how much is that deed — the original, I mean — worth to you, Robin?"

Henry brightened. Now the bargaining was to begin. "Two hundred and fifty thousand, Mr. Krupusa — Krupusiak."

The enormity of it took Krupusiak's breath away. Henry's, too, uttering the figure aloud and at the same time thinking in terms of a quarter of a million. Why, with that much money or anything close to it, he could say the fastest possible goodby to Lennox and Mrs. Taine, take off for any place in the world that fancy dictated . . .

Krupusiak brought him back to earth. "Christ in a wheelbarrow, you out of your mind?"

"Certainly not," replied Henry, sitting up straight, pulling in his paunch, looking dignified. "Hundred acres of land worth twenty-five thousand an acre — ten per cent of it is what I'm asking."

He meant it. He was serious. Krupusiak glowered at him while he did a quick review of his financial position. As always, overextended. The new housing development south of Richmond, the shopping center in Roanoke, the option on that land, a potential gold mine, in Prince William County, the apartment complex in Arlington — God, he was up to his neck in bank loans at the moment. Another few months and he'd have things pretty well squared away but as of right now he could hardly ask for a quarter of a million loan to pay off a blackmailer. Not that he would; not that he'd even consider it under any circumstances.

"Ten thousand," he said. "Ten thousand in cash tomorrow morning and not a goddamn cent more."

"Mr. Krupusiak," said Henry more in sorrow than in anger. "I'll reduce my figure by just that much to show good feeling but that's as far as I'm prepared to go."

Krupusiak's gaze shifted briefly to Breck and Elwood in the rear corner of the room.

" 'scuse me," he said and stood up and went to the men's room.

Breck, after a suitable interval, followed him.

They had the place to themselves. Krupusiak's

instructions were terse. "When the guy leaves—says his name is Patrick Robin—tail him."

"He's got Pennsylvania tags, Mr. K. Even there?"

"I said tail him, didn't I?" Krupusiak snapped and went back to Henry, back to the business of haggling over a figure he hadn't the least intention of ever paying.

It went back and forth. It fell below the two hundred thousand Henry had mentally set as the cutoff point, down to one hundred and seventy-five. There Henry dug in. There Krupusiak felt he had carried pretense far enough.

One last objection seemed valid, though.

"So you bring me the original deed and letter—what's to keep you from holding back photostats?"

"What for? No lawyer would touch them with a ten-foot pole. You know that as well as I do, Mr. Krupusiak. Besides . . ." Henry pushed aside his third drink, rested his elbows on the table and leaned forward to convey his sincerity. "Truth is, I'm getting older, Mr. Krupusiak, never seemed to get ahead much, all I want is a nest egg."

"Sweet Jesus, one hundred seventy-five thousand, you just call it a nest egg?"

"In these times, yes. Enough to live on comfortably but not lavishly—the income from it, I mean—enough to sit in the Florida sun if that's where I decide to settle—"

Not on my money, by God, thought Krupusiak. Except enough to bury you there.

"Y'know, Robin, it's going to take a little time to get this thing straightened out," he said. "I can't raise the kind of money you're asking overnight. I got to borrow it, arrange notes. If you got any thoughts it's just sitting in some bank, forget it. My money works for me."

"Of course," said Henry as one capitalist to another. "Banks don't pay enough interest to let them keep your money for you."

He paused to order his fourth drink and when it came said, "I'm a reasonable man, Mr. Krupusiak, perfectly willing to give you a little time. Let's see . . . this is Wednesday. Shall we say next Monday, April 26? That's almost a week. We meet here at the same time, I with the deed, you with the money. In cash, of course."

"Okay with me. I'll be here." Krupusiak got to his feet and reached for his check but Henry's hand covered it.

"My pleasure," he said benevolently.

"Sure," said Krupusiak and left.

Breck trailed him outside in case there were further instructions. There were none. Elwood remained at their table and paid the check so as to be ready to leave when Henry did.

But Henry was in no hurry. He took his time finishing his drink, afloat on rose-colored clouds.

He didn't notice the big moon-faced man who followed him outside. Or the Firebird tailing him up 95 to his motel in Kingston.

When he turned in at it, Breck, who was driving, went past, came back and sent Elwood in to register for both of them.

They took turns all that night keeping watch on

Henry's car while he, almost a man of means, slept peacefully in his bed.

# 9

He took his time getting started for home the next morning; no point in hanging around Kingston for the best part of a week, money going down the drain for his room and meals; or in taking the chance of running into someone who just might recognize him in spite of the changes the years had wrought. Still, he took his time getting started being in no hurry to get home to his apartment or Mrs. Taine who would be eager to invite him to an unappetizing dinner that was bound to sit heavily on his stomach.

Tomorrow, he reflected over a late leisurely breakfast, he would have to go through the motions of going back to work. Put in an appearance at the office, call the Lennox *Press* and arrange to run his standard ad soliciting property to sell. Perhaps call a few people, too, who had expressed some interest in buying or selling before his trip south.

Next week would be a different story, of course. Once he had his money from Krupusiak he would return to Lennox just long enough to wind up his affairs and take permanent leave of the place. Including, most thankfully, Mrs. Taine.

Henry was too blissfully preoccupied with future plans on his way back to his room after breakfast to notice the blue Firebird parked on the opposite side of the U-shaped building. But once again he did notice, although only subconsciously, the sticker on the rear bumper.

His euphoria persisted on the way home. The Firebird, maintaining a discreet distance behind as he drove north on 95, 495, then 70 to Frederick, Maryland, at no time caught his eye. His unawareness of it continued through a late lunch just over the Pennsylvania border and on north, bypassing Harrisburg.

It was almost dark when he reached Lennox. The street lights came on while he was making his way through the early evening traffic downtown and on into the residential area that brought him to his own door.

Elwood was at the wheel of the Firebird. He would have driven right past Henry except that Breck exclaimed, "For God's sake, El, you want him to spot our Virginia tags? Back up."

Elwood backed up and parked three houses farther down the street, out of range of the street light just ahead.

It shone on Henry unloading his car, making two trips back and forth to deposit his luggage on the front porch. On the second trip he locked his car and disappeared inside the house.

Elwood started to pull forward but was thwarted by another car that swung in to park in front of him.

"Walk past the house, El, and take a look," said Breck who was always in charge of their extracurricular activities.

Henry, in the front hall, had no chance to slip upstairs with his luggage, postponing the announcement of his return to Mrs. Taine. She had her apartment door open before he had closed the door to the vestibule.

"Why, Mr. Fletcher!" She burst out into the hall. "Welcome home. My, let me look at you. What a lovely tan you've got. You look wonderful. A different person from when you went away."

Might have known she'd have her eye at the window, Henry thought resignedly as they shook hands.

"Thank you, dear lady, thank you." He forced warmth into his voice. "I must say I feel like a new man. My vacation did me a world of good."

His luggage included a bag of oranges he had bought for her at the last minute on his way out of Florida. No sense carrying them upstairs now and having to carry them back down again. She had already seen the net bag anyway.

"Brought you a little of the golden sunshine of Florida, Mrs. Taine," he said handing her the bag with a flourish.

Very little of it, she thought, eyeing the bag. Not more than a dollar's worth or so. And not anything personal that called for a little thought. Besides which, she didn't even like oranges. She drank prune juice in the morning. It was good for the bowels.

She hid her disappointment, though, and exclaimed over the oranges as if they were diamonds.

"So kind of you, Mr. Fletcher. So thoughtful to think of me."

"Not at all, dear lady."

She went on to mention the one card he had sent

her. "Such an interesting picture of an orange grove . . ."

She followed Henry upstairs, carrying his smaller suitcase, insisting he join her for dinner. "It just happens that I cooked a nice pot roast today."

He protested that it was too much trouble, had his protests overridden, sighed inwardly and succumbed. Lumpy gravy. Gray mashed potatoes. No way out of it.

"Just give me half an hour, Mr. Fletcher, and it will be ready to put on the table." She started to leave, turned at the door and added, "Breakfast, too, in the morning. Your cupboard must be bare after the time you've been away." She gave him an arch look. "You've got to keep your strength up, you know, with good nourishing meals. We can't have you losing all the ground you've gained on your vacation, can we?"

Henry sought solace in a drink when she was gone. At least he wouldn't have to put up with her much longer. Another month, say, at the most, and he would escape from her forever.

He raised his glass to the prospect. "Here's to the last of Mrs. Taine."

Elwood walked past the house and back. Big, old-fashioned house. Rented rooms, maybe? The house next door had a sign out front, BETTY'S BEAUTY BOX. Neighborhood wasn't as good as it looked coming into it three or four streets back.

A light came on upstairs on the third floor. Robin's place?

He went back to the car and reported to Breck.

"Take a look myself." Breck climbed out of the car. The street was quiet. Most people eating their supper, he thought. He could do with some himself. The sandwich he had carried out from the snack bar while Robin was in the restaurant having his lunch hadn't stayed with him too well. He could do with a drink too.

The quiet emboldened him to go up onto the porch. He could always say he was looking for someone if he got caught, couldn't he?

Front door of frosted glass, dim light inside. The knob turned in his hand. He found himself in a vestibule with a row of mailboxes on one wall. He read the names. Mrs. Edw. Taine, Mr. and Mrs. This or That, only one man, Henry Fletcher, listed by himself. No Robin at all.

Was Fletcher the man they were following? Nothing to prove he had given his right name to Mr. K.

Breck went back to the car. "You stay here," he told Elwood. "I'll scout around and find the nearest motel. After I've signed us in I'll get something to eat and come back and take over here while you go get something yourself."

"What if the guy comes out, though, and takes off somewheres while you're gone with the car? What'll I do about that, Breck? I won't have no way to follow him."

"Don't matter. This is where he lives, we seen him take his stuff in, we know he'll come back. But I don't think he'll go out again tonight. He's an old guy and he's had a long drive today. Reckon he's in now for the night. Okay?"

"If you say so, Breck. What about Mr. K., though? He'll be expecting to hear from us."

"I'll call him from a pay station while I'm gone."

Elwood was left standing disconsolately on the side-walk. The night had turned chilly, much colder than in Richmond this time of year. He turned up his coat collar and wished he was wearing warmer clothes. Exercise helped a little, pacing up and down, keeping an eye on the house.

Nothing happened there, no sign of life until a young couple came out, got into their car and drove off.

Breck returned eventually. Mr. K., he reported, said they were to stay with Robin — or Fletcher, if that was his real name — through tomorrow and find out whatever they could about him. But under no conditions were they to let him catch on to their tailing him. Finally, around three or four tomorrow afternoon, Breck was to call Mr. K. again at his office for further instructions.

"Hell of a note, stuck here," Elwood complained. "Day's growth of beard already and we ain't even got a razor to shave ourself tomorrow morning."

"Find a drugstore and buy one after you eat," said Breck. "Toothbrushes, too, maybe. We don't want people thinking we're hippies. We got to look neat."

"How about other stuff? Like underwear. I been wearing mine three days already. My shirt too."

"Well, wash them out tonight or wear them four. You know Mr. K. don't like us running up big expenses. If he wants us to stay another night then we'll see."

It was nine-forty when Elwood got back. Another half hour and lights began to go out inside the house. At quarter of eleven the third-floor lights went out. A few minutes later Breck and Elwood headed for their motel, stopping at a bar on the way.

At seven the next morning, though, they were back on duty, driving past the house, noting Henry's car still out in front wedged in between two other cars.

Their Virginia plates worried Breck. Broad daylight and all, he said, they stood out more than they had last night.

The problem was solved by parking around the corner below Henry's, taking turns getting out of the car to keep watch.

A little after nine o'clock Henry, having allowed Mrs. Taine to give him breakfast, came out of the house, made a U-turn in his car and headed back downtown, with the Firebird so far in the rear that it barely kept him in sight.

It was a bright April morning with the first swelling of buds feathering the trees. Henry felt so good that he sang off-key to himself, "Everything's coming up roses . . ."

At the lower end of Main Street, well out of the high-rent district, the Firebird almost lost him, braking to a squealing stop, as he turned onto a side street and then into an alley a short distance along it.

Just in time Breck and Elwood saw his car disappear into the alley. They stopped around the corner and waited but there was no sign of Henry.

"Must be a parking place in back and a back door," Breck said at last. "Go past, El, and see."

Elwood drove past slowly. A new brick building on one side of the alley, a down-at-the-heels frame building on the other, refurbished after a fashion with a plate-glass front. FLETCHER AND STEVENS REAL ESTATE proclaimed itself in gilt letters to the right of the entrance, an antique shop to the left.

Elwood nearly hit a parked car as he grabbed Breck's arm and hissed, "Hey, you see that? Fletcher—"

"Yeh, I seen it. But watch what you're doing, El. Just keep going till you find a parking place."

They hung around all morning. There was a convenient bar where they could take turns going in for a beer now and then. Otherwise nothing broke the monotony until Henry emerged at one o'clock, turned in the opposite direction toward Main Street and vanished around the corner.

"Want I should follow him, Breck?"

"Naw, he's just gone somewheres to eat."

Breck already had a phone booth lined up. He looked up the Fletcher and Stevens number, dialed it and asked the man who answered for Mr. Fletcher.

"Sorry, he just went out to lunch. Care to leave a message? He should be back within an hour."

"No thanks, I'll call again."

Breck hung up. So much for smart-ass Henry Fletcher telling Mr. K. his name was Patrick Robin. Take him down a peg or two if he knew how fast Breck had found out his real name, where he lived and what he did for a living.

Breck felt pleased with himself. Mr. K. would be pleased too. No calling him and El stupid jerks this time.

Krupusiak offered no praise, however, when Breck phoned him promptly at three o'clock that afternoon.

All he said was, "Oh," and grunted once or twice. Then, after an interval given to thought, he said, "Well, guess we got what we need on him for now,

Breck. You and Elwood might as well come back and report for work at the construction site tomorrow."

"You don't want us to tail him no more, Mr. K.?"

"What for? We know who he is, where he lives, what he does for a living. We know he'll be back here next Monday. I'll decide what I want you to do about it before then. Stick close to your phone Saturday night. I'll call you then."

That was all. Krupusiak hung up. Breck hadn't really expected praise from him—it wasn't his style—but still, he felt a little flattened as he left the phone booth.

Elwood just said, "Good," when told they could go home.

# 10

Henry returned to Kingston the following Sunday, the day before Miss Bessie Lewis disappeared.

"Property I'm considering as an investment," he explained to Mrs. Taine. And to his partner, Paul Stevens, "Some land down that way an old friend wants my opinion on."

Vagueness about how long he would be gone accompanied both explanations. "Not more than two or three days, I should think, unless something unexpected crops up."

Late Sunday afternoon he registered again at the Kingston Motor Lodge.

"Nice to have you back, Mr. Fitch," said the friendly woman at the desk. "Number 17, the room you had last week? Yes, it is one of the quietest rooms we have, back off the highway, but I'm afraid it's taken. Too bad you didn't reserve it when you were here last week. Historic Garden Week, you know, and tomorrow's Kingston day. Tourists just pouring in. I declare, we'd have had no room at all for you if you'd arrived any later than this."

Breck and Elwood—or rather, Krupusiak—had

been more foresighted. He had told them Friday to reserve a room, assuming that Henry would return to a familiar place instead of shopping around for another motel. Breck had made the reservation by phone from Richmond.

Henry's first move, settled in his room, was to have a drink to give him a lift after the stress of highway travel from Lennox. He had a second drink to celebrate his coming affluence and then sallied forth to treat himself to a bang-up dinner at the best restaurant in Kingston.

He was too excited to sleep well that night and was up early Monday morning, the day Miss Bessie Lewis disappeared. He called Krupusiak right after breakfast from the pay phone nearby and was put through to him immediately.

"About our appointment tonight at Haydon's Run Motel—" he began.

"I'll be there at eight-thirty with your money," said Krupusiak and hung up.

Henry felt snubbed as he hung up himself. It wouldn't have hurt the man to be a bit civil, would it?

Never mind that, though. The big thing was, he'd have his money tonight.

At nine o'clock he drove to the plaza branch of the Kingston National Bank. He took the deed and trustees' letter of thanks out of his safe deposit box, put them in an envelope and tucked it in the inside pocket of his jacket. Then, just to be on the safe side, he put his photostats of them in the box in their stead.

He glanced back at the bank as he walked jauntily out into the crisp sparkly morning. He'd be back there tomorrow. After all, he had paid a year's rent for his box, might as well put his money in it until he decided how he could insinuate it into his life without any awkwardness from Internal Revenue.

He would keep out a thousand or so in cash, though, just to see what it felt like, carrying it around.

Make the last five payments on his car right away, maybe? No, better not. Or at least think about it first . . .

Engaged in these pleasant musings, Henry backed his car out of its slot and swung over into the next lane to drive out of the plaza. Halfway along it his glance fell on a blue Firebird with a sticker — *America Love It or Leave It* — on the rear bumper. A big moon-faced man sat at the wheel and another man, big, burly, was just getting in on the passenger side.

"Oh, my God," Henry exclaimed aloud, the bright day suddenly darkened with recollections of having seen the car and sticker before. At Haydon's Run Motel the night he met Krupusiak there; the next morning outside his motel in Kingston. What about this morning too? Hadn't there been a blue Firebird down the row from him? The bumper sticker wasn't visible from where he was parked himself but surely the car was there, wasn't it?

Instant conviction came to him. Yes, it was. And it had trailed him, with the two men in it, here to the plaza. My God, how long had they been trailing him before that? To the bank, certainly — one of them, no doubt, had even followed him inside and seen him taken out back to the safe deposit room.

No problem for them to put two and two together

97

on that. They'd know he was getting out the deed — acting in all honesty and good faith — whereas God only knew what Krupusiak was up to himself.

Just keeping tabs in case Henry had some scheme in mind to double-cross him? Ridiculous, but the kind of thing a man like Krupusiak might well be capable of.

Indignation sustained Henry as he drove out of the plaza headed toward his motel. Presently, though, as frequent glances in his rear-view mirror showed the Firebird behind him some distance back, uneasiness assailed him. It made no sense that Krupusiak would put not one but two men on his trail just to keep tabs on him. Big, strong-looking men, too, much younger than he . . . What other reason for them then?

The answer came in a burst of fear. They were after the deed. They had orders from Krupusiak to take it away from him by force the first chance they got.

Henry's heartbeat quickened at an alarming rate. It wasn't right, it was an outrage that a man his age should be subjected to such an unnerving experience as this was turning out to be.

His motel lay just ahead but he had second thoughts about returning to it. He could be trapped in his room, robbed of the deed by Krupusiak's henchmen.

His best bet, he decided, was to shake them off, get out of Kingston and then make another call to Krupusiak.

Krupusiak. Henry seethed at the thought of him. He'd tell him a thing or two once he got him on the phone. No more taking him at his word, no more acting in good faith, treating the whole affair as a gentleman's agreement.

He shouldn't have from the start. Krupusiak wasn't a gentleman, never had been, never would be. Crooked as they came, used to cutting corners, a hard-boiled customer.

Well, he would soon find out that Henry could be hard-boiled himself if he had to be.

He drove past the motel entrance and took the turn opposite that would lead him downtown.

The Firebird took the turn behind him.

Henry zigged around this corner, zagged around that one. He beat a red light, went through another that was just changing. The Firebird hung on.

Trouble was, Henry thought, dodging up a side street, Kingston wasn't big enough for this sort of thing. When it was done on TV, the setting was usually a metropolitan area, the rabbit quickly outmaneuvering the hound.

An unfortunate simile. He was no rabbit.

His ducking and circling brought him back unexpectedly onto the bypass near his motel. Like a rabbit returning to its burrow.

That simile again.

He took the next street off the bypass. As he approached the downtown area again he saw the police station ahead, still occupying the old brick building there'd been talk of replacing even in his time. There used to be a cobbled courtyard in back of it with access to it through a narrow alley. Was it still there?

The Firebird was nearly a block behind.

Henry took the corner at high speed, whipped past the police station into the alley and on into the courtyard; into a cul-de-sac, he saw as he braked to a stop. Buildings on three sides of it, a few parked cars and coming up the alley behind him the Firebird, not shaken off after all.

It pulled up right in back of him, blocking off escape.

Henry rolled up the window open on his side and locked the doors as the two men got out and advanced on him.

One of them, with a heavy jaw and menacing eye, leaned against the door. "Got a match, mister?"

Henry rolled the window down an inch. "Sorry, I don't smoke."

"Zatso? Matches right there, mister." A finger pointed to a packet of matches on the ledge over the dashboard.

The other man, the moon-faced one, joined his companion at the window. They stared in at Henry.

His glance skittered around the courtyard. Totally deserted, not a soul in sight. He looked back at the pair helplessly.

A police car came into the alley and pulled up behind the Firebird. The officer driving it blew his horn, stuck his head out the window and said sharply, "What are you-all doing here? Didn't you see the sign back there that says private?"

"Sorry, officer, must of missed it." The heavy-jawed man seemed to be the spokesman, Henry noticed, as he pulled ahead to give the Firebird room to back and turn and clear the way for the police car. He took his time leaving the courtyard himself but it was no use. The Firebird was waiting just past the entrance to the alley.

Henry was on the edge of terror now. What would have happened, what would those goons have done to him if the cop hadn't come along?

He had to get rid of them before he could even think about finding a safe place to phone Krupusiak . . .

He took a turn that said Preston Street. A few doors on a sign outside an old white house said *Historic Kingston Center*; and another temporary sign: *Garden Tour Information*.

Tour buses and cars took up most of the parking lot. There were people, lots of them, milling around, in and out of the building.

It was a walking tour Henry remembered from the brochures thrust upon him here and there. Wouldn't he have a good chance on foot of shaking off Krupusiak's men? He would at least have the advantage of having reacquainted himself with Kingston while they, coming from Richmond, were probably new to it. Once rid of them, he could duck back to his car and get out of town to call Krupusiak.

He found a place to park, bought a block ticket and joined the crowd outside.

The Firebird parked as close as it could get to his car. One of the men went into the center to buy tickets while the other waited near the door.

Henry studied them over the top of the map he had been provided with and felt a fresh burst of indignation at Krupusiak for sicking a pair of big brawny brutes like that onto him. He would have plenty to say about that but it would have to wait.

There was safety in numbers. He tagged along in the wake of a group of women intent on their maps.

Two blocks, three blocks, the 1850 House, first on the tour, classic example of its period, the brochure said.

Krupusiak's men stayed close behind Henry.

He looked at his watch. Just past ten-thirty.

# 11

At ten-thirty Joan Lancaster, Miss Bessie's second cousin on the Lewis side of the family, parked outside 108 Cranston Street, four streets away from Henry, went up the front steps and rapped on the door with the knocker. No answer. She waited, rapped again. Still no answer. She tried the door but it was locked. The third time she rapped harder and longer.

Funny. There was Miss Bessie's car in the driveway and she never went anywhere without it except to Price's, a short walk around the corner.

Had Miss Bessie forgotten the offer she had made yesterday of flowers for Joan's dinner party tonight? "Any time after ten tomorrow," she had said. "I'll be home all morning."

No, she couldn't have forgotten for there was her car.

As Joan looked at it her small frown vanished. Miss Bessie must be out back working in her garden on a pretty morning like this and wouldn't hear anyone at the front door.

Joan went around back. But Miss Bessie's beautiful garden, spring flowers flaunting their colors in well-behaved masses and rows — Miss Bessie kept a sharp eye out for stragglers — was empty.

Perhaps she'd gone inside looking for something? Joan went to the basement door, found it locked, but rattled the knob and called, "Miss Bessie, you in there? Miss Bessie."

No answer. Joan's frown came back. Around to the side door. A bell to ring there. She rang and rang it. Back to the front porch with uneasy thoughts of something having happened to Miss Bessie alone in that big house.

She shaded her eyes with her hands and looked in the front windows. No Miss Bessie in sight lying unconscious or dead on the floor.

Mailbox. A note left for Joan? No.

She hurried around the corner to Price's. But Price Lewis, Miss Bessie's half sister-in-law, shrugged off Joan's concern. "She forgot about you," Price said. "Someone came by, she just popped in the car with them and went off somewhere. You now how scatty she gets sometimes. Why don't you just go home and try again in an hour? Or else go back and cut whatever flowers you want yourself."

"What?" Joan gave her a scandalized look. "I wouldn't dare. You know what she's like. She'd kill me."

"Just a passing thought," said Price. And then, after a pause, "Her and her damn flowers. Her damn everything, for that matter. Go on home, Joan, and stop fretting. I've got to run over to St. James's. I'm late now. I told Matty I'd bring over the cupcakes I baked by ten. I'll be back soon, though, and if you don't get hold of Miss Bessie within an hour, let me know. Incidentally, it wouldn't surprise me one bit to find her over there in the kitchen telling the committee what to do."

Joan laughed but had a doubtful look. "You think so, after what she said on her seventieth birthday? She said she was retiring from all community affairs, including garden week; that she had done far more than her share for years."

"Don't put any money on it, though, that I won't find her over at the parish house," Price retorted dryly.

Joan laughed again and felt reassured as she left for home. But when it got to be eleven-thirty and there was still no answer to her repeated phone calls, anxiety returned. She called Price. "Was Miss Bessie at the parish house?"

"No. No one had seen her all morning. I called her myself when I got back and was thinking just now that I'd better run over and see if she's anywhere around or if her car's still there."

"Call me back," said Joan.

At that particular moment, Henry was sitting at a table in St. James's Parish House glumly munching ham biscuits and chicken salad.

He had reason to be glum, having toured two of the houses at disrespectful speed with no opportunity presenting itself to evade Krupusiak's men. Goons, he corrected himself, sneaking glances at them down the room. They didn't look in his direction at all, devoting their attention to shoveling in with big hamlike hands everything on their paper plates. They looked ridiculous, Henry thought, the only males at their table, surrounded by women. Far as that went, Henry was the only male at his table. There were, he estimated, between twenty and thirty women for every husband, father, or other male connection dragooned into taking the tour.

No hope of escape by the door. The goons were nearer to it and would be after him like a shot. What about the men's room, though? He needed to use it anyway.

Henry muttered apologies to the ladies he had to disturb the whole length of the table and made his way to a hall in back where arrows pointed to the facilities. Out of the tail of his eye he saw the goons start to rise and then sink back when they saw which way he was headed.

The men's room was of one-at-a-time size. Henry bolted the door after him, his gaze going instantly to the window high in the wall. A smallish window, a tight squeeze, but he might be able to climb out of it. First take care of his need, then stand on the toilet lid and open the window.

Perfect, he congratulated himself when he finally got it open and looked out. An old walled graveyard, trees to screen him, grass to cushion the drop from the window, a gate in the wall giving access to the street.

Feet first, of course.

Someone tried the door.

"Sorry, be another minute or two," Henry sang out, one leg going over the sill easily enough but his paunch, even when he flattened it out all he could, giving trouble. He puffed and panted, gradually, a bit painfully eased it over the sill, lifted his head for a look around —

Lounging outside the gate, impassive gaze fixed on him, was the moon-faced goon.

Henry gave him back a haughty stare. Then, grunting with a mixture of defeat and pain got his paunch and the rest of him back in over the sill and down to the floor.

The door was being rattled impatiently. Henry unbolted it quietly, opened it a crack with his shoulder pressed against it for instant closing if the other goon was waiting outside and found himself eyeball to eyeball with an astonished stranger.

" 'scuse me," said Henry and rushed past him.

Outside the parish house where a line was forming for lunch — at least he had taken advantage of the first sitting — Henry looked at his brochure and saw that Cannon Hill was next on the tour, two blocks over and one block up at the top of Gray Street.

Cannon Hill. He had often been there in the old days and remembered it better, perhaps, than any other house in Kingston except, of course, for Miss Bessie's. There had been a charming daughter of the house with whom he had carried on a mild flirtation. He had kissed her one night on the walk out in back that led to Louise Street.

Which meant there were two ways in and out of Cannon Hill. And only a block or so from the one on Louise Street was the alley in back of Miss Bessie's.

Cannon Hill, then, was where he might get his chance . . .

Henry headed for it at a fast pace, wending his way in and out among the tourists going in the same direction.

Krupusiak's men fell in behind.

Fate seemed prepared to smile on Henry at last. Early lunchers and pre-lunchers were converging in great numbers on Cannon Hill whose front door, noted for its fanlight, the brochure said, stood open to receive them.

The wide center hall that ran from the front to double doors in the rear was crowded with people, hostess in green flowered costume smiling a greeting. Double doors in the rear were also open, people out on the porch admiring the miniature boxwood maze and flowering trees in full bloom.

Henry edged his way through a crush of people coming out of the first room on his left. Krupusiak's men were cut off from following him into it by a young man who halted just inside the doorway with a child astride his shoulders.

". . . four hours to polish one of the brass candlesticks," a hostess in blue costume intoned.

Henry slid along the wall. Breck and Elwood, still trying to force their way into the room, were brought to an abashed standstill by green flowers who reproved them gently, "Please gentlemen, if you'll just wait a moment there'll be plenty of room when this group leaves."

"Satinwood chest . . . Hepplewhite . . . Antique mirror very unique . . ."

To use very was redundant, Henry's grammarian self silently chided blue costume as he slid another foot along the wall. Unique was unique and should stand alone.

". . . Bought by one of Mrs. Conrad's ancestors when he was Ambassador to Rome . . . Peking blue china considered among the most beautiful of the known collections . . ."

"Nan! Sarah Lou!" exclaimed a woman so close to Henry that he jumped. "How are y'all? Haven't seen you for ages."

Henry ducked into the next room.

"Waterford crystal chandelier . . ." Hostess here in purple silk, words washing over him. "Chippendale ribbonback chairs . . . Antique American butternut secretary . . . Sèvres vases on the mantel . . ."

Breck and Elwood, eyes glazed with unabsorbed culture, muttered over and over, " 'scuse me, ma'am—if you please, ma'am," but couldn't quite get past a group of matrons standing in the doorway to the next room.

Henry had his chance at last. He skirted the crush spilling out around him, dodging and weaving like a football player, skidded on a rug as he plunged into the rear of the hall and only saved himself from falling by grabbing with flailing arms two ladies whose ample size was all that kept them from being knocked flat on the floor.

"Well, I declare," cried one of them.

"What manners," cried the other.

Henry flew past them, flinging an apology over his shoulder. A moment later he reached the porch, hurled himself down the steps, along the brick walk the endless distance to Louise Street.

The gate stood open to speed him on his way. He tore across the street without looking either way for cars and ran, huffing and chuffing, the whole distance of nearly two blocks to the alley.

The ladies he had almost knocked down were in no mood to step aside for Krupusiak's men when they eventually fought their way to the door. More valuable seconds were lost on top of those already spent in getting this far before the ferocious glint in Breck's eye, the grimness of his outthrust jaw finally made the two ladies draw back.

With Breck in the lead, a step ahead of Elwood, they got out onto the porch just in time to see Henry disappearing down Louise Street. They arrived at the gate just in time to see him turning into the alley.

They darted around a startled group still staring after Henry and took up the chase at lightning speed, Breck issuing instructions, pointing ahead to Cranston Street.

"Stop there at the corner, El, in case Fletcher comes out from behind one of them houses. I'll follow him."

Breck was anticipating Henry's intention. What he meant to do, having the advantage, he thought, of knowing the terrain, was to cut through Miss Bessie's garden—he could only hope he wouldn't run into her—to Cranston Street and around the next corner, showing Krupusiak's goons a clean pair of heels at last.

The time was ten minutes past twelve.

# 12

Five minutes earlier Price called Joan Lancaster. "I can't imagine where Miss Bessie is," she said. "I went over and took a look around. Her car's still there but there's no sign of her. And no answer to her phone."

"I know. I've been calling her myself. I don't know what's wrong, Price, but it's gone on too long. We've got to do something about it. She could be lying helpless in there somewhere. A stroke, a heart attack, a bad fall. She could be . . . dead."

Price's sigh came over the wire. "Reckon we'll have to go look."

"But how will we get in? She's so secretive about where she keeps her spare key—"

"Oh, I have one for emergencies. Come on over and we'll go together. I'd rather not go by myself."

"Better a man, though. Isn't Burney coming home to lunch?"

"No, he's gone to Winchester for the day. You come, Joan, right away and we'll get it over with."

"Okay, I'll be right over."

They hung up. As Joan was hurrying out to her car, Henry was closing the gate to Miss Bessie's garden behind him.

No sign of her, thank God. He kept his pace down to a fast walk in case she saw him from a window, stopped short as he went around the side of the house and saw her car in the driveway. She was home all right. Any moment she might stick her head out the door and demand to know what he was doing in her yard.

He picked up stride going past it but slowed down when he got to the front corner of the house to look around it. There was one of Krupusiak's goons walking back and forth three doors up the street.

Henry retreated to the rear of the building and smothered a groan as he caught a glimpse of the other just moving out of sight past the gate.

God, they had him trapped. They could beat him up, grab the deed, not even give him time to yell for help—if there was anyone to hear him back here in the quiet of the garden.

Come to think of it, why wasn't Miss Bessie outdoors working in it on a beautiful day like this?

Deserted garden, deserted house, doors, windows closed. She wasn't home, the maid wasn't due to arrive yet. The garden tour, of course. Miss Bessie was off somewhere making life hell for someone on some committee.

Henry's unquenchable optimism sped him on his way to the side door. He got the spare key from the trellis, unlocked the door, put the key back and slipped inside, pausing for a moment to listen to the dead silence of an empty house.

It gave him confidence. He moved quickly along the passageway across the hall into the library. He paused again, facing row on forbidding row of Grandfather Pemberton's law books, unopened, untouched for years except for an occasional dusting.

Henry reached up to the third row from the top, pulled out the third volume from the left — *Blackstone's Commentaries* — thrust the deed far back behind the next volume and restored the one he had removed to its place.

Perfectly in line, nothing to show any disturbance, as he stood back to look at the shelf. If Krupusiak's goons caught him now, he would turn out his pockets on the instant to prove he didn't have what they were after.

Perhaps — more optimism — if he just stayed where he was for a while they would think he had somehow eluded them and give up the chase.

He sat down in Grandfather Pemberton's chair to wait them out. His watch said twelve-fifteen.

Miss Bessie, seated in the dining room of the Prince George Hotel a short distance away, would have found her watch in agreement with Henry's if she had looked at it just then. Instead, she was trying to decide whether she would order Crab Norfolk or Chicken à la Prince George for lunch.

"They're both delicious," she told her chance-met hostess, Laura Weldon from Westmoreland and Laura's two Maryland guests who were going to take the tour with her. "Simply delicious. But I guess I'll have the Crab Norfolk myself . . . Yes, I'll have a drink first. An old-fashioned. I certainly need it after the morning I've had. The insurance man from Richmond appearing on my doorstep from out of the blue at ten o'clock wanting me to go down to Haydon

County with him straight off to show him where my accident happened two weeks ago . . ."

Price came walking around the corner to Cranston Street just as Henry sat down in Grandfather Pemberton's chair. She didn't notice Elwood watching from the corner of Louise Street up above; nor did Joan Lancaster when she drove around it a few moments later in her car.

Elwood, however, noticed them; and which house they met at, his gaze on them until they went out of sight going around to the side door.

He hoped Breck wouldn't let them see him back in the alley.

"I hope everything's all right," Joan said uneasily as Price inserted her key in the door.

"Oh, of course it is," said Price. "This is just to make sure."

Henry had warning of their approach. A window must be open somewhere for even though he was on the far side of the house he heard their voices as they greeted each other outside.

He rushed out into the hall, eyes sweeping over the scene for a hiding place. A lamentable lack of closets, only one he knew of downstairs. It wouldn't do. The basement was the best bet.

He shot back the bolt and was halfway down the stairs when he heard the side door open and footsteps in the passageway.

A few moments later, moving on tiptoe, he was squeezing himself behind the monster stove in the old kitchen, rubbing his nose to keep from sneezing in the cloud of dust he had stirred up.

Then there was nothing to do but wait.

The time was twelve-twenty.

Joan and Price called Miss Bessie's name as soon as they were inside the door and looked at each other uncertainly. The stillness bothered them.

"Shall I look upstairs while you look down here?" Joan asked.

"All right," said Price. "But try not to disturb anything. You know what Miss Bessie's like. If there's even one rug out of line or a door open an inch farther than she left it, it will be the first thing she'll notice."

Tentatively, feeling like intruders and yet half fearful of what they would find, they began to search the house for Miss Bessie.

Price, with no beds to look under and only one closet to inspect, finished first, ending up in the kitchen. It was in its usual perfect order except for Miss Bessie's breakfast dishes and small coffee pot left in the sink. At least she'd had breakfast that morning, Price thought. But what could have become of her since?

There was still the basement, Price reminded herself, looking around the room in bafflement while Joan's footsteps echoed overhead.

If the door to it was bolted—and Miss Bessie said she was careful about that—there'd be no need to search it at all.

Price went to look. The door wasn't bolted. Was Miss Bessie down there, perhaps fallen down the stairs?

Price opened the door almost dreading to let her glance go to the foot of the stairs for fear that she would see an unconscious form lying there.

But there was only the rug spread out neatly below the bottom step.

"Miss Bessie?" She called her name twice and then went slowly down the stairs.

Henry, squeezed behind the stove, had begun to get cramps in his legs. He couldn't imagine what all the activity and calling of Miss Bessie's name signified and didn't even dare change position as he listened to it. When Price opened the door to the old kitchen, came in and glanced around, he was ready to faint from fright, having no way of knowing that she was looking for Miss Bessie in plain sight, unconscious or dead on the floor, not hiding behind the stove.

She didn't go anywhere near it but left quickly, closing the door after her and going across the landing into the cellar calling, "Miss Bessie . . . Miss Bessie?"

Another few moments and Henry, with infinite relief, heard her going back up the stairs and the door closing above. He came out from behind the stove gasping over the crick he got in his back as he straightened up, rubbing his legs to restore circulation.

He was too old for such goings-on he mumbled to himself in self-pity. And all the fault of that slippery, double-crossing Krupusiak. By God, he'd get a good piece of Henry's mind once he had a chance to call him.

It was now close to twelve-thirty. In the kitchen overhead Price and Joan were conferring on their next move.

"Reckon we'll have to start calling Miss Bessie's friends and neighbors to see if they know where she is," said Price. "We'll make a list beginning with the closest ones."

"Better begin with Miss Leila Couch then," Joan said. "She's closest of all to Miss Bessie."

They made up a list including on it with some hesitancy Tess Maitland, Miss Bessie's next-door neighbor and longtime enemy.

They began calling, one on the phone while the other looked up numbers. Five or six calls covered the obvious names before moving on to less likely ones. But no one had seen or heard from Miss Bessie or knew of any plans she had for the day. After the first few calls, Price's offhand approach—"Trying to get hold of Miss Bessie, just wondered if you'd seen or heard from her today"—took on a worried note. "Can't imagine what's become of her. Her car's right here but she's left no word—she just seems to have disappeared."

There were widening ripples of concern in Miss Bessie's circle; suggestions of other people to call; of checking all the houses on the garden tour in case Miss Bessie had been pressed into last-minute service somewhere. There were offers to help with the telephoning; requests to be informed if there was any news.

The word was spreading fast by the time Iris arrived at five minutes past one: Miss Bessie Lewis had disappeared.

Iris was no help. Every name she suggested, every possibility she brought up had already been taken into account.

It was Price who said, "I don't think we can let this go on any longer. We'll have to notify the police."

"I've been thinking the same thing myself," Joan agreed.

But Iris shook her head, a doubtful expression on her dark face. "Miss Bessie wouldn't put up with police messin' around in her house. She'd have a fit."

"We know that as well as you do, Iris, but what else can we do?" Price demanded. "We can't just let it go on and on."

Iris shrugged. "Up to you, Miss Price. Only remindin' you how Miss Bessie will take on over it."

They were in the kitchen. Iris went over to the sink and started stacking Miss Bessie's breakfast dishes in the dishwasher. "She sure left in a hurry not to do this herself, the way she likes things so. But if you ask me, it's still no cause to—"

"Yes, it is," Price interrupted crisply and picked up the phone and called the police.

At one-twenty a police cruiser pulled up in front of the house. As the cop in it went to the door, Cranston Street stirred into life, neighbors peeping out from behind curtains, phone calls spreading the news of Miss Bessie's disappearance still farther afield.

Elwood retreated hastily around the corner of Louise Street when the cruiser arrived and beckoned Breck away from his sentry duty in the alley.

"The fourth house down from the corner," he reported. "You reckon they caught Fletcher hiding out in there or something?"

"Could be. Go back and see if the cop brings him out. But keep out of sight yourself all you can." Breck set an example for his colleague by removing himself from the alley to lounge negligently against a tree near the entrance to it.

Henry pricked up his ears when he heard the front door open and close and new footsteps overhead, heavier sounding, more like a man's.

Who was it, though? There seemed to be a regular convention going on up there. He listened apprehensively at the door. Male voice, all right. He moved back closer to the stove ready to squeeze in behind it again at a moment's notice.

The cop was given a résumé of the situation by Price and Joan, beginning with Joan's arrival at the house three hours ago for her promised flowers, going on through unanswered phone calls, the search of the house, the futile inquiries among friends and neighbors.

Iris, having stated that she knew nothing about Miss Bessie's disappearance, washed her hands of the whole affair by going upstairs to do Miss Bessie's room.

"Can't imagine," Price and Joan said. "It's not as if she just forgot about the flowers and suddenly took it into her head to go off somewhere. Her car's right outside . . ."

The police officer nodded. He was only too familiar with Miss Bessie's car. Parking tickets, warnings for going through red lights, tickets for reckless driving, speeding—it had all been going on for years, leading to indignant descents on the police station that the whole force had come to dread. To say nothing of complaints from Miss Bessie about stray dogs ruining her garden, motorcycles roaring past her house, and a variety of other complaints, including a threat last winter to sue the police department over a crumpled fender resulting not from any fault of hers,

Miss Bessie maintained, but from careless placement of a barricade around a broken gas main.

Yes, he had noticed Miss Bessie's car outside, the officer said with neutral expression. Wasn't it a little soon, though, to feel alarmed over her absence? After all, their inquiries couldn't have included everyone she might have gone out with, could they? For instance, couldn't some out-of-town friend here for the garden tour have stopped by and asked her out somewhere?

Price and Joan hadn't thought of that. While they looked at each other weighing it, the front door opened and Miss Bessie burst in upon them crying, "What's going on here? What's the police car doing out in front of my house?"

# 13

Dead silence as the three, clustered near the stairway, looked at her.

"Well, Price, Joan, speak up one of you," she prodded sternly. "Can't I go out for a few hours without coming home to find police" — a withering glance at the cop — "tramping all over my house, neighbors wondering what's going on — speak up, I said!"

Price was the first to recover. "It was just that we were worried about you, Miss Bessie," she began. "You weren't here, you hadn't left any note when Joan came for the flowers you promised her this morning — "

"You mean to say that just because I let a trifling thing like that slip my mind you brought the police in on me?" Miss Bessie's pudding face turned scarlet with anger.

"But, Miss Bessie, your car was outside, you didn't answer your phone, Joan and I got more and more worried — "

"Ridiculous!" Miss Bessie snorted. "Joan, why on earth didn't you cut whatever flowers you wanted and go home and mind your own business instead of stirring up all this ruckus?"

"Cut your flowers myself, Miss Bessie? Why, I'd never—" Joan broke off at a warning glance from Price, and changed the subject. "Where did you go this morning? If you'd only thought to call me . . ."

The cop was waiting patiently for the right moment to interrupt the discussion and take his leave. But Miss Bessie was planted squarely in the doorway and God knew what she'd say to him if he asked her to step aside.

He might not have existed as far as she, glaring at Joan Lancaster, was concerned.

"I didn't think to call you, I didn't have time to, because everything happened in such a rush," she snapped. "I had the adjuster from my insurance company in Richmond at my door at ten o'clock. Just happened to be in Kingston, he said, and wanted me to go down to Haydon County with him—you know, that little accident I had down there two weeks ago when that idiot from Haydon Court House cut right in front of me when I was making a left turn?—and the insurance adjuster wanted me to show him exactly where and how it happened because it wasn't quite clear, he said, from the report I made to my agent here . . ."

As Miss Bessie paused for breath the cop took a step nearer the door.

"Anyway," she resumed, "I went with him right away, not stopping for a thing, wanting to get it straightened out that the accident wasn't my fault, not a bit of it.

"Took us over an hour and when we got back I

asked him to drop me off downtown and who should I run into in front of the Prince George but Laura Weldon from Westmoreland with some friends of hers she was taking on the tour . . ."

The tour. The cop felt vindicated in his theory about Miss Bessie's disappearance.

"To make a long story short, Laura invited me to have lunch at the hotel with her and her friends—perfectly charming, both of them—and then they dropped me off here. Or rather, thank heaven, down at the corner, not noticing that the police car was right out front. I did, of course. I didn't know what I was going to walk in on. Where's Iris? Why'd she let you-all start this nonsense, police sticking their noses in—Iris!" Her voice rose to a shriek. "Where are you, Iris?"

Henry shrank into himself hearing that voice overhead.

Iris came leisurely down the stairs. Miss Bessie, arms akimbo, broad dumpy figure still blocking the front door, confronted her irately.

"What got into you, Iris, letting Miss Price and Miss Joan start all these carryings-on? I declare, you should have more sense if they haven't."

"Tried to stop them," Iris retorted coolly. "Said you wouldn't like it, Miss Bessie, but they was bound to go ahead, fretting away because they didn't know what became of you. Searched the house upstairs and down, even the basement—"

"Basement?" Miss Bessie turned on Price and Joan scathingly. "You think I was Houdini going down there and bolting the door after me?"

"It wasn't bolted," Price said sharply having put up

123

with all she was going to. "That's why I—"

"Of course it was bolted," the older woman interrupted. "I bolted it last night before I went to bed and didn't touch it this morning."

"The door was not bolted, Miss Bessie." Price spaced her words evenly. "That's the only reason I went down there."

Happily, Henry couldn't hear what was being said or his nerves would have been shattered completely. He could catch a word now and then but mostly just the voices. Above all, Miss Bessie's.

"Then Joan must have unbolted it without your knowing it."

"I never went near the door," Joan declared.

"You must have forgotten it last night, Miss Bessie," Price said, refusing to be intimidated.

"No indeed! I'd never in the world forget it."

"But you forgot I was coming this morning," Joan pointed out.

"Entirely different." Miss Bessie swept down the hall to the passageway to look at the door herself.

It gave the cop a clear path of escape but he couldn't bring himself to take it. It was a pleasure to see Miss Bessie being taken down for once.

"Door's bolted now." Miss Bessie came back up the hall.

"I bolted it," said Price. "But it wasn't before."

"Then someone's been in the house since I left. A thief, a burglar—"

"We searched it from top to bottom," Joan said. "Not a sign of anyone."

"But the door could hardly unbolt itself."

"Miss Bessie," Price spoke on a weary note, "you

must have forgotten to check it last night."

"How could I? I made my usual rounds same as I do every night of my life . . ." Miss Bessie's voice was as loud as ever but failed to carry conviction. She knew that her listeners were thinking that she couldn't be absolutely sure, performing a routine chore, her mind, perhaps, on something else . . .

"Want me to search the house again before I go, Miss Bessie?" The cop was enjoying himself.

"No indeed." Authority flowed back into Miss Bessie's voice. "Just go this minute, please, and get that dreadful Black Maria of yours away from my front door."

"But thank you for coming," Joan and Price said, walking out to the porch with the policeman.

The phone rang as they went back into the house. Miss Bessie whisked away from them to pick it up in the library.

"Hello? Oh, Leila," they heard her say. "No, of course I didn't disappear. A lot of nonsense Price and Joan got into their heads. Next thing I know, I'll have to ask permission every time I leave the house . . . No, not at all. Just happened the insurance adjuster came this morning . . ."

Price and Joan exchanged shrugs and went out to the kitchen to ask for a pair of scissors. Iris raised her eyebrows.

"I'm cutting the flowers myself," Joan said firmly and went out into the garden with Price lending moral support.

The phone kept ringing, Miss Bessie getting more and more irritated by inquiries about her disappearance.

125

There was no call from her next-door neighbor Tess Maitland.

No one remembered how many years had passed since they, never very friendly, last spoke to each other or just which fund-raising luncheon led to their last encounter.

It took place in a kitchen, Tess Maitland carving a ham, Miss Bessie back and forth criticizing.

"Too thick, Tess, much too thick. Who wants to eat slabs of it?"

"Miss Bessie, I'm carving the ham. Will you let me alone?"

"But you're ruining it. It should be thin, thin. Grandfather Pemberton always said ham should be sliced so thin you could read a newspaper through it."

"Get out of here, Miss Bessie!"

"No, Tess, I can't just walk away and see you tearing chunks out of a beautiful ham like that." Then, voice rising, "There's a knack to carving—"

"Miss Bessie—"

"You don't have the knack, Tess," voice rising to a shout. "Let me do it. Give me the knife."

"Don't tempt me, you interfering old bitch, or I'll give it to you where it will do the most good." Tess Maitland advanced on her brandishing the knife. "Get out of this kitchen right now and don't you ever even speak to me, let alone shout at me again as long as you live!"

Miss Bessie, almost in fear of her life, fled.

And so there was no inquiry on her well-being that afternoon from Tess Maitland.

Elwood reported to Breck. "Old bag went in the house a little while ago—like she owned it, y'know?—

126

and now the cop's just left but he didn't have Fletcher with him. Think it didn't have nothing to do with him, Breck?"

Breck shook his head. "Stands to reason there's some connection. Take a walk past the house, El, see what the number is and if there's anything going on."

Elwood went off to carry out orders. Came back to report that the house number was 108 and that there was nothing going on, far as he could see.

"What's the name of the street?"

Elwood looked blank. "It don't say. Just the number."

"Chrissake, there's a sign at the corner. Go look."

"I wasn't thinking." Elwood gave him a sheepish grin, went up to the corner and returned with the information that it was Cranston Street.

Breck got out a notebook, licked a stub of pencil, wrote 108 and asked, "Cranston spelled with a K or a C?"

"C," said Elwood after thought.

"C-r-a-n-s-t—" Breck wrote. "An i or an e at the end?"

Elwood hesitated, then said, "e."

Breck wrote e and n, frowned in thought as he put away the notebook.

"I can't figure it out, El," he said at last. "Cop there, Fletcher running into the alley. He's got to be around somewheres. But whyn't the cop nab him?"

Breck paused again for thought. "God, what if he got away somehow through the next yard or something."

"Couldn't. You seen the thick hedge. Six feet high at least."

127

"Maybe there's a thin spot somewheres. Or he went out the front way and you missed him somehow. Look, you better hightail it back to that place where we bought the tickets, El, and see if his car is still there. Stay with it if it is. I'll try to cover both the alley and the street."

"Which way do I go, Breck? I'm kind of twisted around."

"My God, El, see the sun off to your left? It's moving south. You go that way. You'll find the place."

"Okay." Elwood set off, not running exactly, moving at more of a fast trot.

# 14

Henry, meanwhile, stayed close to the stove leaning against the wall beside it shifting from one leg to the other as both began to ache, a twinge here, a throb there. Small varicosities, hardly noticed most of the time. Natural at his age, he said. Too much weight, his doctor said.

He listened intently to every sound from above. Footsteps in the hall, front door closing, car starting up out in front. Just women's voices after that. Whoever the man was, he had left.

The phone rang. Shortly thereafter the side door opened and closed and two women appeared in the garden. Henry spent an anxious interval keeping out of sight of the windows while they moved about cutting flowers. Then they vanished around the corner of the house.

He heard Miss Bessie's voice next — a softer voice — wasn't it Iris, the maid she had yelled at the other day? — responding.

Presently he heard the distant hum of a vacuum cleaner, water running somewhere, then the telephone again. It seemed to ring every few minutes.

Henry felt it was safe to tiptoe across the room and sink into a wooden chair, not really comfortable, but giving his legs a rest. He was hardly settled, though, when he heard the bolt shoot back above, the basement door open and light quick steps on the stairs.

He leaped to his feet, rushed over to the stove and squeezed himself in behind it, nerves quivering, sweat pouring down his face.

But at the foot of the stairs, the steps turned the other way into the cellar. It was the briefest of trips, the door closing a moment later, the footsteps going back up the stairs.

Miss Bessie's bellow echoed down from above. "Iris, make sure you bolt that door now, hear?"

"Yes ma'am."

Door closed, bolt shot home.

Henry crept out of his hiding place, mopping his face with his handkerchief, needing a few minutes to collect himself before he could give his attention to the predicament he was in with the door bolted above.

He had meant to stay until dark, until Krupusiak's goons gave up hounding him and took themselves off. He had hoped that Miss Bessie would go out somewhere this evening after the maid left. Or, if he was very lucky, out to dinner again as she had that night last week. If she stayed home, he had resigned himself to waiting until she was in bed and asleep. He had then intended to slip upstairs to the library, get the deed out from behind the law books and leave by the side door just as he had the other time.

The damn bolt on the basement door hadn't entered into his considerations at all. It should have, but it hadn't.

But now it was bolted, probably for the night, and he was trapped here in the basement. He certainly couldn't go out the back door and leave it unbolted top and bottom behind him. The best he could do was climb out one of the windows after dark and hope no one would notice very soon that it was unlocked.

But what was he to do then unless Miss Bessie went out tonight—hang around until the small hours before he tried to sneak in the side door and get the deed back?

Damn the woman and her bolts and locks!

Henry fumbled automatically for his pipe, got it out, put back in his pocket. He could hardly smoke here.

He heard water running again overhead, a reminder of how thirsty he was, his throat dry with dust from the stove as well as all his exertions.

There was that half-bath in what used to be the maid's quarters across the landing. He couldn't take a chance on it, though. Iris had already made one trip downstairs.

The telephone kept on ringing overhead. Couldn't all be social. Miss Bessie must still be running some committee or other. Something to do with the garden tour, maybe.

The calls were about Miss Bessie's disappearance. Her voice got sharper with each one. "Utter nonsense," she exclaimed over and over. "All Price and Joan's fault. Calling people, calling the police, making a perfect fool of me . . ."

Time dragged on. Henry kept dozing off, finally woke himself up with a loud snore that made him start; that could almost, it seemed, be heard upstairs.

He got to his feet and stretched to ease his muscles. He was as thirsty as ever and shortly became aware of an even more urgent need. His bladder, he reflected sadly, wasn't what it used to be. Why, there was a time when he could go all day and not even know he had one . . .

He cocked his head to listen. The maid no longer right up over him, just distant sounds that placed her and Miss Bessie somewhere else in the house.

There was a sink in that half-bath across the landing. There'd be a glass, no doubt, and he could let water just trickle into it so as to make no sound in the pipes. Couldn't flush the toilet, of course, but still, there was the sink . . .

He felt better when he came tiptoeing back. A little past five-thirty his watch said. He had dozed nearly all afternoon. Better unfasten the window catch before dark.

He looked out. Shadows lengthening in the garden, no sign of Krupusiak's men in the alley. Night would fall before seven.

No, it wouldn't. He was forgetting that daylight saving time had started Sunday. Almost two hours to go yet.

Henry sat down and dazed again, chin on his chest. This time he was awakened by the crash of something hitting the floor overhead. A shout from Miss Bessie at the front of the house, Iris shouting back, "Just dropped a skillet, Miss Bessie. Just dropped it, is all."

Quarter past six. Miss Bessie wasn't going out to dinner. The maid was getting it.

The light was fading in the basement but the sun still shone outside. God, wouldn't it ever get dark?

The next moment Henry was struck by the mournful reflection that however the spirit might soar the body was earthbound. Specifically, in the present instance, his stomach clamored for food, uninterested in future plenty; and nervous stomach that it was, it needed a drink too. Lord, what he wouldn't give for a good stiff shot!

He smothered a belch. Hunger always made him gassy.

Sounds from above indicated that Miss Bessie's dinner was now being served.

Dinner cleared away, darkness coming at last, the maid leaving by the side door calling out, " 'Night, Miss Bessie. See you tomorrow."

Silence overhead, Henry tiptoeing out to the landing to listen, then the phone again, Miss Bessie, from what he could hear, picking up on the library extension.

This was the moment to get out, her voice bound to cover any unavoidable sounds associated with his exit through the window.

At least the brick walk outside meant that he left no footprints to betray his presence. It was worth scraping his hand as he lost his balance and fell on one knee.

He meant to leave by the alley. He would have run right into Breck, patrolling around the corner to

Cranston Street and back, except that Breck had halted at the entrance to the alley to light a cigarette just before Henry peered over the gate. He saw the red tip glow and fade, and ducked back into the garden, all the way back to the house.

He halted then in despair. One of the goons still on guard in the alley, the other must be out in front.

But when he went to look, what seemed to be the one from the alley came around the corner from Louise Street, walked as far as Miss Bessie's and turned back, his cigarette butt a flicker of sparks as he dropped it in the gutter.

Just one of them now, Henry thought, watching from the shelter of Miss Bessie's car. Spelling each other, perhaps. As soon as the goon got back around the corner he would be able to leave.

A few minutes later he was safely on his way, hugging the shadows from street to street as he covered the distance, nearly a mile, to the Historic Kingston Center.

The building was in darkness as he approached it but lights on in the parking lot revealed two cars still there, his own and the Firebird. He circled around through darkness in back of a printing shop next door to reconnoiter. Dismay seized him as he saw the other goon seated behind the wheel of the Firebird.

He was not going to be able to get to his car tonight.

He tottered off to the Prince George Hotel, obliged to retrace his steps over half the distance he had already come. It was crowded with tourists but a cancellation had made a third-floor room available.

Henry paid in advance, having no luggage. He freshened up as much as he could with a pocket comb his only grooming aid and descended to the dining room for drinks and dinner.

His physical well-being restored, his spirits improved, too, the Micawber side of him back in control. Wait until eleven o'clock before returning to Miss Bessie's, he thought, scout around to avoid the goon outside, and if she had gone to bed, take a chance on trying to get the deed back. If he was very quiet, if he took his shoes off at the door, no reason he couldn't get in without her, in her front bedroom, hearing him. Burglars got away with it, didn't they? If they could get in and out of houses and rob the sleeping occupants without being caught, why shouldn't he? No harm, anyway, in giving it a try.

He had a brandy to bolster his courage after dinner. Still only ten o'clock. With an hour to kill, he had another.

At quarter of ten Miss Bessie phoned Price to berate her once again for her part in the day's events.

"Calling everyone in town about me," she fumed. "Making a fuss over nothing, saying I'd disappeared. Can't imagine what got into you, Price. My phone hasn't stopped ringing since, people wanting to know what happened to me. Don't know when I'll hear the last of it. Worst of all, getting the police here. You know all the trouble I've had with them."

Price tried to defend herself but Miss Bessie's rapid-fire recital of grievances overrode her.

"Couldn't have happened at a worse time either. You know I have to go to court day after tomorrow."

Price had forgotten. "That ticket you got for driving the wrong way on Cranston Street last month?" she said faintly.

"Exactly. Just for going past three houses on my own street. You know perfectly well I refused to pay the fine and demanded a trial that's been twice postponed. That no-account, chickenhearted policeman who gave me the ticket ain't been able to appear, they keep telling me. Huh! Ashamed to, I shouldn't wonder. He better be there Wednesday, though, or I'll give that prosecutor—imagine Jim MacLaren that I've known since he was in diapers prosecuting me!—a good piece of my mind. But that's neither here nor there. I just hope that another time you'll have better sense, Price. After all, you're going to be fifty years old next birthday, it's time you learned to use your head."

It took Miss Bessie until after ten o'clock to finish putting Price in her place.

Getting up from the phone, she was ready for bed. She'd had a tiring day, all that foolishness going on, people in and out, all those phone calls to answer. She would take a walk around the garden first to make sure that wretched cat from up the alley wasn't in her flowerbeds again and at the same time get a breath of fresh air. She stopped in the kitchen to get her flashlight out of a drawer and went out the side door.

The fresh air, as she went around in back, turned out to be polluted with cigarette smoke.

"Who's there?" She flicked on the flashlight and caught Breck, paused at the gate, squarely in its beam. "Who are you and what are you doing hanging around here?" she demanded imperiously.

He started to turn and run, thought better of it in case the old bag roused the whole neighborhood by screaming.

"Just out for a walk before bedtime, ma'am."

"I don't know you." Miss Bessie kept the flashlight on his heavy-jawed face. "You live around here?"

"No, ma'am. I'm a tourist. I'm staying downtown." Breck put up his hand to shield his eyes. If she had asked for the name of a hotel he couldn't have supplied one.

"Tourist?" She lowered the flashlight a little. "You don't look like one to me. But whoever you are, sir, you're trespassing. This is private property and you have no business here."

"Sorry, ma'am. Didn't know. Wouldn't of—" Breck melted back into the shadows.

Miss Bessie, sputtering to herself, returned to the house, forgetting, after all, to look for the neighbor's cat.

She then made her rounds to assure herself that everything was locked up for the night and went upstairs to bed.

Breck retreated from the alley, deciding that the old bag's attitude made it plain there was no point in hanging around any longer. If Fletcher had been hidden anywhere in her house or yard she would have flushed him out long ago. In spite of the cop who'd been at the house, wasn't it possible that they'd been wasting their time all these hours with Fletcher gone from the area ever since he gave them the slip on the

137

tour? El wasn't too sharp. He could have missed him cutting through the yard and out onto Cranston Street.

At least he hadn't vanished in his car. If it had been gone from where it was parked, El would have driven right back to report it.

Even so, Breck wasted no time on his way to the Historic Kingston Center and was relieved to see that Henry's car was still there. Immediately, though, he got into an argument with Elwood over his having somehow missed Henry. What with Elwood's vehement protests that this couldn't have happened, it was a good ten minutes before they settled down to practical matters, Breck saying he would call Mr. K. from the nearest pay station and forage for food while Elwood stayed on guard.

Miss Bessie's house was in darkness when Henry made a cautious approach to it at eleven o'clock, making sure neither of the goons was in sight before he stole into the yard and watched and waited for another interval before going up to the side door.

He located the key and unlocked the door, turned the knob slowly, carefully, and then discovered that it was held by a chain.

Damn it to hell, he hadn't even noticed that there was one attached to it!

He wasn't cut out to be a burglar, that was his trouble.

Try to force the chain or work it loose with a nail file? He didn't dare, didn't know how much noise it would make.

He put the key back on its nail and crept away.

The night had turned cold. There was some consolation, returning to the Prince George, in the thought that Krupusiak's men would spend an uncomfortable night waiting for him at the Historic Kingston Center. If they did. If they hadn't already given up and gone back to the motel.

He considered calling a cab and driving past the center to see if they were still there. But it was too much trouble. He needed a nightcap and bed. At his time of life he had to guard his health.

# 15

At six o'clock that night Krupusiak gave up waiting at his office for a call from Breck and went home to dinner. He still couldn't quite believe that he hadn't heard a word from him or Elwood since a little after nine that morning when Breck had called from some shopping center to report that Fletcher had gone into a bank there; and the next moment hung up saying he had to get back to the car, Fletcher having just come out of the bank with a long envelope that he was putting in his pocket.

The goddamn deed, of course.

After dinner—and it was all Krupusiak could do to be half-way pleasant to his wife and kids at the table—he announced that he had work to do and retired to the room that his wife called his study and he called his office. He did have some overcost figures he wanted to check but he couldn't concentrate on them, waiting for the phone to ring, his private line, not an extension of other phones in the house.

His phone rang around nine but when he snatched up the receiver it wasn't Breck or Elwood. He cut the call short and sat there at his desk scowling at the instrument.

Twelve hours now since Breck had called him. A simple assignment to get a piece of paper away from a bumbling old fool like Fletcher and they hadn't been able to carry it out. Play it by ear, he had told Breck. Don't pull a gun on him if you can help it. Don't rough him up any more than you have to. But if he gives you any real trouble, beat the hell out of him. Even if he ends up in the hospital he won't dare squawk. He'd have to admit blackmail if he did.

Those were the orders he had given Breck. They'd had twelve hours to carry them out and not a word from them. A simple, straightforward assignment that a high school kid could handle and somehow the stupid jerks had screwed it up.

Jesus, it had got so a man couldn't depend on anyone these days.

At ten o'clock Krupusiak's wife came into the room. "Are you going to work much longer, Joe?"

"Dunno."

"Well, I think I'll go up to bed now." She came over to the desk and kissed him good night. "You work too hard, dear," she said.

"Good night," he said.

Breck called him at quarter of eleven.

"You get it?" Krupusiak asked.

"Well, no, not yet, Mr. K. Lot of things has happened—"

"Like what?" Krupusiak's voice was dangerously quiet.

"Well, the way it turned out . . ." Breck told the story defending himself as best he could.

"You should of seen them houses he took us to, Mr. K. Packed with all these garden tour ladies and

141

everything. We couldn't pull a gun on him or knock him down in front of them, could we? Or knock them down, neither, chasing the old bastard when he took off, could we?"

At this point Krupusiak exploded. Breck held the phone a little away from his ear while he waited for the storm to blow itself out.

When Krupusiak ran out of expletives and began to repeat his lurid opinions of Breck and Elwood's brains, ancestry, judgment, ability to carry out any job beyond digging a ditch — and by God, he doubted if they could even do that — Breck felt it was safe to say, "Look, Mr. K., I know how you feel, I feel terrible myself, the way it turned out, but what do you want us to do now? It isn't like we lost Fletcher for good. El's right over there in the parking lot now keeping an eye on Fletcher's car. He's got to come back to it sometime. You just want us to stay around there somewheres until he does?"

"No, no need to hang around there any longer. You'll only scare him off. Go back to your motel and get some sleep to see if it will sharpen your wits any. You can check on the parking lot in the morning. He's got your car spotted by now so hire another one. Use it to go to his bank and see if he shows up there. Send Elwood to City Hall. They'll have a city directory. Tell him to look up 108 Cranston Street and find out who lives there. Have him call me as soon as he gets the names. Then he can try keeping an eye on the house and the parking lot too."

"But what if Fletcher gets his car when we're not around?" asked Breck. "And then don't go back to his motel? How would we know where to look for

142

him?"

"You wouldn't," Krupusiak replied, and added on an exaggerated note of patience, "but he still wants to sell me that paper, that deed, don't he? Which means that sooner or later he's got to get in touch with me again to set up another meeting."

"Oh," said Breck. "Reckon you're right, Mr. K."

"Well, that's it then for tonight," Krupusiak said. "And for God's sake, Breck, see that you don't get everything all screwed up again tomorrow."

He hung up. Breck hung up disconsolately and set out in search of a restaurant. When he got back to the center with sandwiches and coffee he told Elwood how mad Mr. K. was and that they'd have to do better tomorrow.

When Henry took a cab to the center the next morning he was ready to have the driver whisk right past it if there was any sign of the Firebird or its owners. But there were only tourists, not so many as yesterday. Henry paid off the cab, got into his car and removed himself from the vicinity with all possible speed.

Success in eluding Krupusiak's men encouraged him to make a survey of his motel parking lot. Again there was no sign of the Firebird or its owners. He stopped at the office to announce that he was checking out, went on to his room and was packed and gone in a matter of minutes.

It seemed prudent to seek new quarters beyond the environs of Kingston. Henry drove ten miles north of the city and registered at a motel just off I-95. It was a small motel but offered the convenience of a restaurant close at hand and a gas station with a

143

public phone booth outside.

Henry wasted little time settling in. He hung up his raincoat and other suit and took a straight shot from the bottle in his suitcase to steady his nerves before he called Krupusiak. Then he was off to the phone booth to make the call.

There was a slight delay over the connection, Krupusiak, when he heard it was Mr. Patrick Robin calling, telling his secretary to switch the call to an outside line.

He took the offensive immediately. "Well, Mr. Robin, you didn't keep your appointment at Haydon's Run Motel last night," he said.

The effrontery of it! "Don't try to pull that on me, Mr. Krupusiak," Henry retorted. "You didn't keep it yourself. Instead, you sent those thugs of yours, those goons, after me—you had them with you at Haydon's Run Motel last week—you never meant to pay for the deed—" Henry stammered with indignation as he went on to the question of good faith, a bargain made to be kept on his side but never, obviously, on Krupusiak's who had intended all along to rob him of the deed.

Krupusiak cut him short. "You got the whole thing wrong, Robin. I had the money ready, I waited for you an hour last night at Haydon's Run Motel but you never showed."

"Are you trying to tell me you sent your goons along yesterday just to keep me company?"

Krupusiak shifted ground. "I'm a businessman. Let's say I sent them along yesterday to keep an eye on you to make sure you were acting like you said, in good faith. I don't take anybody's word for anything.

144

My boys lay a finger on you, Robin?"

"No thanks to them that they didn't. If I hadn't got away from them—"

"Maybe they exceeded their instructions a little. All I said to them was, keep an eye on Mr. Robin, see he's on hand to deliver the goods like it was agreed to."

There was no talking Krupusiak down. Smarter men than Henry could have told him that. Henry almost, but not quite, believed him before he was done.

"So why don't we pick up where we left off, Robin," Krupusiak said at last. "Meet me tonight instead of last night at Haydon's Run Motel. Eight-thirty, like we said."

"No indeed," replied Henry. "That won't do at all. This time we'll meet in Kingston in the lobby of the Prince George Hotel where there'll be people around and where I won't have to go outside into any parking lot where your goons might be waiting to exceed their instructions again. At the Prince George I can just retire to this little alcove and count the money and then get the deed out of the hotel safe where I'll arrange to leave it and put the money in instead. No need for me to worry then about your goons."

Very foxy thinking, Krupusiak reflected. But Fletcher wasn't as smart as he thought he was. A jerk, in fact, not to put the whole thing in writing—a letter to be opened in the event of his death and stashed away in that safe deposit box he had rented. Rocks in his head not to have thought of it. All he was worrying about, of course, was Breck and Elwood grabbing the deed off him. It hadn't even occurred to him, apparently, that he might get himself knocked off over it.

Well, Krupusiak didn't want to see it go that far himself. On the other hand, one hundred and seventy-five thousand was a motive for killing that stuck out a mile.

If worse came to worse, that was.

"Since that's the way you want it, the Prince George Hotel, it's all right with me," Krupusiak said. Then, to give himself a little more time, "But shall we make it tomorrow night? I've got an appointment tonight that I can't break."

"That's all right with me," Henry replied, needing time himself to retrieve the deed from Miss Bessie's library. He had second thoughts, in case he couldn't get hold of it that soon and added, "As far as I know now, that is. If it turns out I can't make it, I'll get in touch with you and we'll see what other arrangements we can make."

They left it at that.

Elwood called Krupusiak while he was still talking to Henry. His secretary put the call on hold until Henry hung up and then switched it through.

"I got the name, Mr. K.," Elwood said. "A Bessie C. Lewis lives in that house."

"No one else listed there?"

"Just that one name. I wrote it down."

"Okay. Get back on the job, keep an eye on the house and the parking lot."

"Will do, Mr. K."

Krupusiak wrote the name down himself, Bessie C. Lewis. He stared at it and sat back in thought. Who did he know in Kingston who could give him information and at the same time keep his mouth shut?

It took him only a moment to come up with Grattan, resident manager of the townhouse complex Devco had built in Kingston three or four years ago. He was a local guy who should know something about Bessie C. Lewis. Keep his mouth shut, too, knowing which side his bread was buttered on.

Krupusiak pressed his intercom button and said to his secretary, "Get me Grattan at Two-Mile Road Court in Kingston."

Presently Grattan came on the line. "Morning, Mr. Krupusiak."

"Morning. Look, Grattan, d'you know a Bessie C. Lewis at 108 Cranston Street?"

"Sure do. Reckon everyone in Kingston does." Grattan chuckled. "Real character, Miss Bessie is, always sticking her nose in something."

"Busybody old maid, eh?"

"Well . . ." the other hesitated. "Seems as if I've heard she was married once years ago. Some fellow from out of state. Didn't take. He left town, she got a divorce and resumed her maiden name. Before my time, though. Miss Bessie's no spring chicken."

"Uh-huh." Krupusiak had Henry placed in an instant. Ex-husband, got his hands on the deed somehow.

"Old girl got money?"

"Oh yes. Loaded, I'd say. Beautiful old house too. Been in the family for generations."

"Prominent family?"

"Oh yes. Most of them over in Pine Hill Cemetery now but real important people in their day."

No question about it, Krupusiak thought. None at all. Charles Sheffield, teetotaler, who had put that

147

clause in the deed was Miss Bessie Lewis's ancestor. Even so, it would do no harm to have Breck take a run over to the cemetery and check out gravestones.

"Well, Grattan, thanks for the information," Krupusiak said. "It's for a friend of mine. Something he's got going that she wants to invest in. It's still not settled, though, so keep it under your hat."

"Sure will. But tell your friend he'd better watch his step, any dealings he has with Miss Bessie. She's sharp as a tack where money is concerned and she'll sue over anything that doesn't suit her. Or sometimes, from what I've heard, just for the hell of it, just to stir things up."

"Oh," said Krupusiak in a fading voice. "I'll pass the word on." He hung up, all thoughts of dealing with Miss Bessie Lewis himself vanished. Plenty of money, couldn't be bought off cheap, made a hobby of lawsuits.

The grim look on his face deepened. That son of a bitch, Fletcher . . .

The gloves were off now. He'd get that deed from him however he could, alive or dead. The choice would be up to Fletcher.

When Breck called a few minutes later from the shopping plaza Krupusiak told him to forget about watching the bank.

"Go to Pine Hill Cemetery—no, you stupe, I don't know where it is, but you can ask, can't you?—and look for Sheffield and Lewis graves. Start with Charles C. Sheffield—"

"Wait a minute, Mr. K., let me write them down." Out came Breck's notebook, stub of pencil, his tongue to moisten it. Names were spelled for his benefit and written down.

"Got 'em, Mr. K."

"Let me know what you find out." Krupusiak dropped the receiver in its cradle. A moment later a new thought burst into his mind and he snatched it up again. But he was too late. Breck had hung up.

There was no way to reach him or Elwood until they called again to tell them to forget everything else and concentrate on Miss Bessie Lewis; that Fletcher would have to show up there sooner or later because that was where the deed was now, hidden in his ex-wife's house ever since he got away from Breck and Elwood yesterday. Stood to reason. He knew the house well, had some way of getting into it, figured the deed would be safer there than carrying it around on his person with Breck and Elwood on his tail.

Now he would have to start keeping his own watch on the house, looking for another chance to get into it when his ex-wife was safely out of the way.

Then, if Breck and Elwood could work out some way to get in themselves, it would be a better place for them to grab the deed off Fletcher than anywhere outside.

If it couldn't be worked out that way, they'd have to figure out something else. One way or another, by God, they had to get that deed away from him.

# 16

Miss Bessie stayed home that day. She worked in her garden all afternoon — Breck narrowly missed having her catch him in the alley again when she first went outdoors — and had friends visiting her in the evening after dinner.

From Henry's point of view, therefore, the day was totally wasted.

After his call to Krupusiak he drove back to Kingston, parked his car at the lower end of Cranston Street and made his first cautious reconnaissance of the one hundred block.

No sign of the Firebird. Miss Bessie at home, her green Plymouth in plain sight from two houses away. She hadn't been home yesterday, it was true, when her car was in the yard, but that wasn't likely to happen two days in a row.

There were, as usual, a number of cars parked on the street. Most of the houses, a hundred years old or more, were built on narrow city lots and lacked space for garages. Once Henry had made sure the Firebird was nowhere in view, he paid no attention to any of the other cars, least of all to the gray Dodge Dart parked just below the corner of Louise Street.

Breck and Elwood ducked down the moment they recognized his portly figure in the distance, hatless white head in need of a haircut, untidy locks blowing in the breeze.

"How far away did you leave my car, El?" Breck inquired inching an eye over the dashboard to keep track of Henry's slow careful approach.

"Three streets over," Elwood replied.

"Hope to hell he don't start checking the whole neighborhood for it," said Breck watching Henry crane his neck this way and that at parked cars as he drew near the one hundred block.

But Henry was still just looking for the Firebird. The possibility of a rented car didn't occur to him; it was an expense he never felt prosperous enough to indulge in himself.

As soon as he saw Miss Bessie's car in her driveway he turned back the way he had come.

Breck pulled out from the curb a little to keep him in sight but gave him a long head start in his Chevy II before taking up the pursuit.

Henry had no destination in mind as he left Cranston Street behind him. It was eleven o'clock and there was no point in returning to his motel when he meant to check 108 again within the hour to see if the coast was clear yet. And so he drove at random until he saw a bowling alley ahead. He had been missing his weekly bowling night, his only form of exercise, lately. Might as well bowl a few games now, he thought, turning in at it. As good a way of killing time as any. If he had glanced up the street on his way into the building he would have seen the gray Dart

151

stopping at a parking meter some distance away. But it didn't catch his eye; it wasn't the Firebird.

"Maybe you should scout around for a phone, El, and let Mr. K. know we picked up Fletcher again," Breck said shutting off the motor.

Elwood cast a glance over the area, made up of shabby little houses. "Don't see none around here," he said. "Unless they got one in the bowling alley. They prob'ly have."

"Well, you can't hardly go in there and use it," Breck said. "Maybe that's all Fletcher went in for himself. Or to go to the men's room."

He paused in thought. "Leave it go for now, El. We can call Mr. K. later."

Soon after twelve o'clock Henry came out of the bowling alley and headed back to Miss Bessie's, this time circling around by Louise Street, open to two-way traffic, and driving past 108 Cranston, sighing in defeat when he saw the Plymouth still parked in the driveway.

Not a hope now of getting in the house all afternoon, with the maid due at one o'clock. He would have to wait until she left around seven-thirty. Maybe he'd have better luck then. Maybe Miss Bessie would go out tonight.

He drove downtown and lunched economically on a hamburger and a bottle of beer. The restaurant was across the street from a movie theater. He could kill some more time there. Anything was better than staring at the four walls of his motel room.

Breck and Elwood, after a suitable interval, followed him into the theater, settling into seats well away from the one Henry had chosen.

The movie was *Cromwell*. Since their combined knowledge of history, English or otherwise, could be passed through the eye of a needle, they dozed through most of it, waked up now and then by the battle scenes.

Henry, who couldn't remember when he had last been to a movie, succumbed to a few snoozes himself before it was over.

At five o'clock, though, he was back on Cranston Street. Miss Bessie's car still in the driveway, no sign of life until the maid left shortly before seven-thirty. A little later three elderly ladies arrived. When Henry walked past and looked in they were seating themselves around a card table. No chance of getting into the house tonight. Go back to his motel, have a couple of drinks for a pick-me-up and eat at the restaurant nearby. If he had no better luck tomorrow he would just have to postpone his meeting with Krupusiak.

Breck and Elwood lost him at the first downtown traffic light. A parked car pulled out so suddenly that Breck had to slam on his brakes to avoid hitting it. He blew his horn angrily at the driver but by the time he got around the car the light, green for Henry, had turned red and traffic was already moving across his path.

"Hop out quick, El, and run to the corner. See if you can see if Fletcher turns off anywheres."

Elwood hopped out and ran to the corner but was shaking his head when the light changed and Breck swung over to the curb to pick him up.

"I couldn't tell," he said. "There was too many cars crossing at the next light and all."

They had lost him for good. There were too many streets, too many turns he might have taken. And at night one taillight looked very like another.

Henry was at no time aware of their following him as he drove back unmolested to his motel.

Krupusiak took calmly enough the news that they had lost Henry again.

"It don't matter," he told Breck who was braced for another outburst such as had followed his earlier call to report that he hadn't been able to figure out who was related to who on his trip to Pine Hill Cemetery. "Like I told you before, that deed's in the house. Fletcher'll be back there first thing tomorrow morning."

But that was a matter of interpretation. For Breck and Elwood it meant rousting themselves out of bed at six o'clock and being on duty in the vicinity of 108 soon after seven.

For Henry it meant reaching Cranston Street at nine o'clock.

For Miss Bessie it meant leaving the house at nine-fifty to appear in Municipal Court at ten.

She had scarcely backed out of her driveway before Breck went through the gate into her garden, keeping in the shelter of the tall hedge and hiding himself in the densest shrubbery he could find close to the house.

Henry was less precipitate, remembering from the old days Miss Bessie's habit, that age would not have improved upon, of forgetting something she meant to take with her and rushing back home for it.

So he lit his pipe and waited a good fifteen minutes in his car, parked up above the house.

Around the corner on Louise Street, Elwood waited to carry out Breck's orders. After Henry's arrival, he had moved the Dart up nearer the corner so that by stretching his neck he could see the rear end of Henry's car.

He was worried, though, over keeping as close to him as Breck had said he should. Only one woman in sight at the moment, walking down Cranston Street, no one else around, not as many parked cars as there might have been to give him cover, how was he to keep real close to Fletcher without being spotted?

Henry solved his problem for him when he finally tapped out his pipe in the ash tray and got out of his car. After a last look around for the Firebird, he walked briskly down the street to 108 and around the corner to the side door.

He didn't even look back once, Elwood noted with relief, keeping a station wagon between them as he crossed the street in Henry's wake.

Henry rang the doorbell three or four times. He rocked back and forth on his heels, whistling softly to himself "I'm Sitting on Top of the World" as he waited for it to go unanswered. Then he reached into the trellis with a negligent air and took out the key.

Crouched in the shrubbery, Breck watched him unlock the door, hold it ajar while he put the key back, wait until the car had passed by before he went inside.

A moment later, after a quick glance around, Breck shot out of the shrubbery and up to the door himself. He had the key in his hand when Elwood came strolling into view, his casual air enhanced by the cigarette he was smoking.

Breck beckoned him over and at the same time slowly, quietly turned the key in the lock, put it back on its nail and eased the door open.

"Put out that cigarette," he hissed over his shoulder.

Elwood took a last hurried drag and tossed it away as Breck slipped inside. Then he followed in Breck's footsteps, stealthy as a red Indian except that the Indian would not have had Elwood's morning cigarette cough. It overtook him unexpectedly, a deep spasm of it, while he was trying to shut the door after him without making a sound. He clapped his hand to his mouth but it came out in a wheezy strangled gasp loud in the silence.

Henry, who had stood in the passageway and listened to that silence before he made any move at all, had just started into the library when he heard the wheezy noise behind him.

He whirled around, cried, "Oh, my God," when he saw them and ran faster than he had in years for the front door.

But they were even faster. They brought him crashing to the floor as he reached for the knob, then dragged him up onto his feet.

"Where's that paper?" Breck demanded.

Henry, the wind knocked out of him, was too dazed for the moment to speak. He shook his head uncertainly.

"Where is it — that paper, that deed?" Breck slammed him back against the wall. Elwood kicked him in the shins.

Henry got his breath back, wrenched one arm free. "Let me go, you thugs, you goons!"

He ducked the full force of the punch Breck aimed at his jaw, reached down to grab the rug Elwood was standing on and yanked it out from under him. Elwood landed on hands and knees, came up with a murderous look on his face and dived at Henry.

Breck regained his grip on him. There was a brief wrestling match, a flurry of punches, rugs in a tangle, a chair knocked over, before they got Henry back against the stair railing and began hitting him with sledgehammer blows that came too fast for him to ward them off.

"Where's that deed? Where is it, you sneaky old bastard . . ."

Voices fading, blood running down his face, ribs hurting so that he could hardly breathe, one of them holding him as his struggles weakened, a search of all his pockets, more oaths and questions, his head jolted back with a furious blow that almost cut off his awareness of anything. Then from what seemed like far away, a voice saying, "Take it easy, El. How can he tell us what he done with the paper if you knock him out cold?"

Paper. The deed. He'd have to tell them. He couldn't take any more of this . . .

A car turned in onto the driveway.

# 17

Elwood ran into the dining room to peek out a window, came running back. "Oh Jesus, we got to get out of here, Breck. It's her, the old bat who lives here."

Old bat. Miss Bessie. She was home, they were saying. The thought of it restored Henry's waning consciousness like a glass of cold water thrown in his face.

He braced himself against the bottom stair, struggled to his knees and then to his feet. He swayed back and forth looking blearily at Breck and Elwood as they opened the front door and walked out with firm step as if they had been in the house on legitimate business.

Henry rubbed his eyes trying to clear his vision. One of them, though—he touched it gingerly—seemed to be swollen half shut.

Breck and Elwood were not within Miss Bessie's range of vision as she got out of her car in the driveway. The slam of the car door closing started Henry on an unsteady run toward the front door himself, fear of being caught by Miss Bessie greater than his fear of Krupusiak's men.

He tripped over a bunched-up rug and almost fell; then almost fell again as he bent down to straighten it out and the pad underneath, touched with sudden sharp awareness that he couldn't leave the hall looking like that, rugs kicked about every which way, for Miss Bessie to find. She would have the police swarming all over the place in no time and demand so much protection that he'd never be able to get near it again.

He staggered frantically back and forth, straightening out rugs and pads, picking up the chair that had been knocked over, listening the while for her key in the door.

What was keeping her?

He heard her voice just then yelling to someone outside. Oh God, what now?

Henry opened the front door a crack and peered out. Krupusiak's goons were walking up toward the corner of Louise Street. A woman with a bag of groceries under her arm and other bags on the front seat was getting out of her car across the way listening to some story of Miss Bessie's, indignantly told, about going to court that morning and having her case postponed again.

Henry drew back and closed the door in despair. Miss Bessie had walked out to the end of her driveway. She might come in the front door. Even if she didn't, he couldn't escape by that route. The other woman would still be outside getting her groceries out of her car. She would see him, call Miss Bessie or challenge him herself—

He pressed his hands to his sore aching head. One

came away with blood on it from the deep scratch or cut on his face that burned at a touch. He reached for his handkerchief and saw that a pocket was almost ripped off his jacket. He must look a sight. He couldn't show himself on the street until he had cleaned up a bit.

He would have to hide in the basement again, get to the sink down there to wash his face, find a pin somewhere, maybe, to fix his pocket.

A quick look out the dining-room window showed Miss Bessie still talking but moving back up the driveway, indicating that the conversation was nearly over.

It was now or never if Henry was to get down into the basement before she came in the side door. He broke into a shambling trot, all he was equal to, moving toward his sanctuary. Even that much effort made him dizzy and bending down to fumble with the bolt on the door made him dizzier still.

He straightened up clutching the frame for support. Miss Bessie's voice sounded louder now, almost as if from right outside.

Henry reached for the railing, closing the door after him, plunging down the steps, head whirling, losing his balance, falling, falling into sudden painful oblivion as he hit the landing at the bottom of the staircase . . .

The first thing that caught Miss Bessie's gimlet eye as she came into the house was the bolt drawn back on the basement door. Just like the other day when they had all tried to tell her she must have forgotten to bolt it the night before. Well, she'd let them talk her into half-believing it then but not this time! She

160

had looked at the door when she left the house less than an hour ago and it was bolted then.

She flung it open, turned on the light and screamed at the top of her lungs when she saw Henry spread-eagled at the foot of the stairs, the rug that had cushioned his fall bunched up under him.

She clung to the railing and went down a few steps for a closer look. White-haired man, blood on his face, eyes closed — he was dead!

For all her strong character, Miss Bessie couldn't bring herself to go down any farther. She rushed back up the steps and began screaming again. "Help, help, there's a dead man in my basement — a dead man — dead —"

Her voice cut through the wall of darkness that enclosed Henry. The slam of the door, the sound of the bolt shot home brought a groan to his lips. He stirred feebly while Miss Bessie, her cries dwindling for lack of breath, ran outside to summon the neighbor she had just been talking to.

But the neighbor had gone into her house and there was no one else in sight. Miss Bessie shrieked at a man going by in a car but he didn't hear her. When two children appeared and stared at her curiously, she turned back indoors. No sense running around like a chicken with its head cut off. Call the police.

She made her way into the kitchen and sank trembling onto the nearest chair before reaching for the phone. This time she was entitled to use the emergency number without their getting uppity about it as they had on other occasions.

While she was dialing the number, Henry was pulling himself upright supported by the railing and after a moment straightened out the rug with one foot.

Miss Bessie's voice at top pitch penetrated his daze. "Yes, a dead man in my basement, that's what I said . . . Of course I'm sure. You think I don't know a dead man when I see one? . . . Right away? Well, I should hope so."

The police, Henry thought, coming quickly to himself. They'd be here any minute. The window he'd got out before . . .

Somehow he reached it. Afterward he didn't know how he had done it, crept through the old kitchen, got the window open, got out it and closed it quietly after him, got through the garden, the alley, up Louise Street and around the corner to his car.

If Miss Bessie had gone to the back window she would have seen him reeling through her garden, resting for a moment against the gate before he could make the immense effort required of him to walk with some semblance of steadiness the rest of the way to his car. Providence was on his side at last, however, keeping him from coming face-to-face with anyone until he reached it and climbed in behind the wheel.

Breck and Elwood, who had moved the Dart farther up Louise Street, couldn't believe their eyes when they saw Henry emerge from the alley without Miss Bessie in pursuit.

But she was still sitting in the chair by the telephone waiting for the police. She felt her age all of a sudden.

The cruiser swept up Louise Street, turned onto Cranston Street past Henry slumped in his car and pulled into Miss Bessie's driveway.

There were two officers in it this time prepared to cope with a dead man. The sight of them hurrying up the front steps galvanized Henry into further effort. He got out his keys, started the motor and drove away.

Breck and Elwood set out after him.

Miss Bessie met the officers at the door.

"Come in," she said. She recognized one of them from the other day. Well, she thought triumphantly, she'd put him, Price, and Joan in their place. His sidekick too — hadn't she had a run-in with him once about a parking meter that didn't work? Now they would all have to admit she wasn't just a silly old woman imagining burglars behind every door.

"This way," she said leading them to the basement door. "He's down there, dead at the foot of the stairs." Her voice shook slightly as she conjured up the image of the sprawled body. "I don't want to see him again. I'll wait in the kitchen."

One of the policemen unbolted the door and opened it. They both looked down and exchanged frowning glances.

"Did you say the foot of the stairs, Miss Bessie?"

"Yes."

"There's no dead man there. There's nobody there at all."

"What are you talking about? Of course there is. White hair, blood all over his face, rug bunched up under him — "

"Rug's perfectly flat now, ma'am."

"Never mind about the rug. The body has to be there. I saw it with my own eyes." Miss Bessie rushed out of the kitchen to the head of the stairs, looked down, then up at the policemen in utter bewilderment.

"It's gone," she said. "But how could it be—unless someone took it—"

"But what would anyone want with a dead body, Miss Bessie?"

The question went unheeded. Her bemused gaze was fastened on the foot of the stairs, uncluttered by a corpse of any sort.

For once, perhaps for the only time in her life, Miss Bessie was speechless.

## 18

Fringe benefits. Thus did Henry describe to himself the irritating little extra problems that tend to cluster around a major one like tugs around an ocean liner coming into port. Such as, in his case that morning after all that had happened to him at Miss Bessie's, his realization that he was very low on liquor as well as being almost out of pipe tobacco too; to say nothing of needing some sort of ointment for the cuts and bruises sustained in his encounter with Breck and Elwood.

So he had stops to make before he could retreat to his motel room. First the men's room at a gas station where he washed the blood from his face and improved his battered appearance as much as he could. Then he had to brave stares at the ABC store to buy a bottle. His third stop was at a drugstore to take care of his other needs. The pharmacist expressed solicitude — or curiosity — openly.

"I ran into a door," Henry told him with great dignity.

At last he was free to go on to his motel. A straight shot enabled him to undress and lower himself into the tub for a long hot soak followed by treatment of his wounds and a cold pack for his eye, now swollen almost shut. After two aspirins and another straight shot he crawled into bed to sleep for the rest of the day.

Breck and Elwood had no trouble tailing him to his motel or in deciding, after the stops he made, that he wouldn't be leaving it for the rest of the day.

Breck called Krupusiak from the same phone booth Henry had used.

Krupusiak listened to his recital of events in stony silence but at the end his restraint vanished.

"Why did you have to crowd him like that?" he demanded through gritted teeth. "Didn't it enter your goddamn stupid heads to give him a few minutes to get hold of the deed before you went in after him?"

"We just wanted to make sure what he did."

"So you went in like a herd of elephants to scare him off."

"Oh no, Mr. K., nothing like that. Couple of mice was more like it. Only it just happened Fletcher going into this room turned around and seen us." It seemed politic to edit out any reference to Elwood's chronic cigarette cough.

"What kind of a room?"

"Like a liberry. Lot of bookshelves with books on them."

"Books," said Krupusiak. "So that's where he hid it. In or behind one of them." After a moment's thought he added, "He'd pick old books that no one ever looked at."

"Expect he would." Breck tried to sound ingratiating.

But Krupusiak's voice rose heatedly. "So then when he tried to get away you and Elwood had to beat him up! How in God's name did I ever get stuck with a pair of dumb creeps like you? You saw what room he was going into. You saw the books. Still, it never entered your stupid heads to just let him go and then look for the deed yourselves?"

"But the old bag came right back anyways," Breck defended himself. "She would of caught us."

"You mean you couldn't have handled one old woman between the two of you? Suffering Jesus, is that what you mean?"

"Reckon we didn't think of it like that, Mr. K. It all happened too fast. What d'you want us to do now? Leastways, we know where Fletcher is. We could get into his room—"

"No, don't go near him," Krupusiak snarled. "Let him make the next move. He'll be calling me. God only knows how I'll handle him after what's gone on, but he's still got to contact me."

"Maybe he got that paper, though, after me and El left. It was a good ten minutes or more before he come out through the alley."

"Maybe he did but I doubt it. He was in no shape for anything but to get away himself after the beating you gave him. He came out the alley, you said, from the back yard. Seems like he went down cellar to hide. We don't know. All we know is, the old girl saw him or something and called the cops. Chances are, the deed's still in the house."

Krupusiak paused again for thought. "Could be,

the best bet is to bypass Fletcher altogether and go after the deed ourselves. Let me think about it some more, though. Call me at home tonight. Meanwhile, rent another car — don't use your own car at all — and split up. Let Elwood stay with Fletcher and you keep an eye on the house. But don't try anything on your own, hear? The way you've screwed things up, I want to do some more figuring on it myself. Because next time, by God" — Krupusiak's tone turned ominous — "it better go right. I'll have both your asses if it don't. I didn't get to where I am today, Breck, taking excuses for performance. Just bear that in mind before you make any more mistakes." Krupusiak, getting mad all over again, banged down the receiver.

Breck went unhappily back to Elwood.

At 108 Cranston Street, the policemen, under Miss Bessie's adamant eye, searched the house. They turned up no body, no evidence that there had been one, warm or cold, on the premises.

Except for the unlocked window in the old basement kitchen. Miss Bessie's shoebutton eyes lighted up at the sight of it. "That's the answer," she said. "They got him out that way."

"But first of all, how'd he get in upstairs, Miss Bessie? The door couldn't be unbolted from this side."

"Well . . ." She hesitated. "Oh, I know. I left one of the library windows open a little way. The screen was hooked but that wouldn't stop them. That's how they got in."

"Who's they, ma'am?"

"Why, the dead man and his confederates, of

168

course." Eyes snapping, "His murderers who pushed him down the stairs and killed him."

"If he really was dead," said the braver of the two policemen.

"Of course he was! Think I don't know a dead man when I see one?"

"But if he was just knocked out, Miss Bessie, couldn't he have come to and got out the window by himself?"

"He was dead, I tell you!"

"When did you last check this window to make sure it was locked?" It was the braver policeman again, veering off on a new course.

"Recently. I check all the windows down here or else Iris does regularly."

"How recently was the last time, ma'am?"

Miss Bessie glared at him. "You expect me to name the exact day, a trifle like that?"

Raised eyebrows from the policemen said the window might have been unlocked for months.

"You think I'm making this whole thing up?" Miss Bessie's voice went shrill. "You think there never was a body at the foot of the stairs? You think—?"

"No indeed, Miss Bessie, not at all. We just wondered . . ."

They escaped to search the garden and the alley. Assurances came next. They would check with the neighbors—

Dumpy figure drawn erect, quivering with rage, face showing a remarkable resemblance to Queen Victoria when she was not amused, Miss Bessie said acidly, "You going to ask if they've seen the body of a man that vanished from my house lying around their yards or something?"

"No, ma'am, nothing like that. Just if they've seen any strangers around, things like that."

"Don't bother. A dead man in my basement, just let it go, and take your big flat feet out of here."

They went, though, to neighbors up and down the street, Miss Bessie watching, spluttering to herself, from a window.

The braver one came back to report the one small bit of information gained; about an hour ago a woman up the street had noticed two big men she had never seen before going around the corner to Louise Street. But neither of them had white hair, matching Miss Bessie's description.

"Hardly. Unless dead men have started walking around."

"I meant it couldn't have been him, ma'am, while he was still alive." The policeman's voice was polite but chilly. He'd had all he was taking from Miss Bessie this time.

He got himself off her front porch with assurances of further checking and the suggestion that if anything else turned up she had only to call them. Meanwhile, he said, police cruisers would be asked to keep an eye on her house.

"Idiots. Nincompoops," Miss Bessie stormed to herself as they drove away. "They're telling each other right now that it was all my imagination. Calling me an old fool, no doubt."

She phoned Price to unburden herself. But Price wasn't home. Nor Joan Lancaster. They had no right not to be when they had started this whole business bringing the police in on her the other day. Now there were two false alarms charged up against her.

Only this second one wasn't. And why should she, a responsible citizen, taxpayer, helping to support such incompetence, put up with it?

She wouldn't. She didn't have to.

A few minutes later Miss Bessie marched out of her house, got into her car, defiantly turned the wrong way to reach Louise Street, the route she had been deprived of by the new system of one-way streets.

Thoughts of this additional wrong inflicted upon her added fuel to her anger. She parked as close as she could get to the police station and sailed inside demanding to see the chief.

The desk man, mindful of his superior's statement not to let it happen again, the last time Miss Bessie cornered him — over boys playing ball in her alley and breaking a window, wasn't it — fobbed her off on the captain to whom the cruiser officers had already made a report on going to her house.

The captain listened patiently, asked questions as tactfully as he could, repeated the assurances his subordinates had already given her and at last eased her out of his office, she making it plain that she was still unsatisfied.

Funny, though, he reflected when she was gone. Miss Bessie was a tyrant, a busybody, an eccentric nuisance but she still had all her buttons, far as he could tell. And in her many complaints in the past, there was usually some kernel of fact among the chaff.

He sent for one of the policemen who had answered her call and went over her story with him again. There could have been a man in her house who had knocked himself out falling down the stairs trying to escape when she arrived home, the policeman conceded. But there was no evidence whatsoever that he had broken in—he could have just walked in if she left a door unlocked—and no traces of his presence unless you counted the basement window which might well have been unlocked for months.

"You can tell she doesn't use the basement much, sir," the office added. "Bolts the door at the head of the stairs and figures that takes care of it. Which it probably does, I reckon."

"That call Monday—"

"Wasn't from Miss Bessie, sir. It was her sister-in-law, Mrs. Burnett Lewis, saying she'd disappeared."

"So we can't blame that on Miss Bessie."

"No, sir."

They talked a little longer about it. But lacking anything to support Miss Bessie's story about all they could do, the captain said, was to keep a close eye on the house.

Miss Bessie couldn't believe her eyes when she got back to her car. A parking ticket stuck under the windshield wiper!

She rushed back into the police station where the desk man took the brunt of her fury.

When he could at last get a word in he said, "From what you tell me, ma'am, I'm afraid you parked in the space reserved for the county sheriff. There's a sign—"

"I didn't see it."

"I'm sorry, but it's right there in plain sight. A yellow line too. If you'll just go outside and look — "

Miss Bessie went. The sign was there and the yellow line . . .

Even so, she tore the ticket up. It was just too much.

# 19

*Readers Forum, Kingston Dispatch,*
*April 29, 1971*

To the Editor:

Again I call the attention of the citizens of Kingston to our local constabulary whose gross inefficiency is fast becoming a disgrace to the community.

Not that they don't do very well when it comes to writing out parking tickets, issuing summonses for minor traffic violations and engaging in other forms of petty harassments. They seem to have plenty of time and manpower at their disposal for activities of that nature.

But a major crime is a different story. Let no citizen seeking the protection that is one of his basic rights look to them for assistance.

An intruder in the house, a dead body in the basement? Don't bother us with such trifles, they will say. We haven't got time for them. We're too busy writing out parking tickets.

How long will this continue?

BESSIE C. LEWIS
108 Cranston Street

# 20

"But I don't know what else the police could do about it, Miss Bessie," Burney Lewis said that Wednesday evening when, after numerous phone calls, she finally reached him and got him over to her house with Price to hear about the dead man in her basement and the perfunctory routine of the police investigation.

"At least they're keeping a watch on the house," Burney added. "Police car went by while Price and I were on our way over."

"Huh," Miss Bessie snorted. "What good would that do me if I was being murdered in my bed?"

"Would it make you feel easier to have us spend the night with you?" Price inquired.

The older woman quickly shifted ground. "No indeed," she said. "Not a bit necessary. I'll lock everything up tight and I have a phone right by my bed. I hear the least sound and I'll get the police here — for all the good it will do me. At least" — she tossed her head — "I made sure Kingston people know what kind of protection they're getting. I wrote a letter to the *Dispatch* this afternoon and had Iris take it right over to make sure it gets in the paper tomorrow."

Burney and Price exchanged resigned glances but said nothing. No one could control the ready flow of Miss Bessie's pen.

Burney was fourteen years her junior, the only child of the marriage of his widowed mother, Mrs. William Burnett and Miss Bessie's widowed father, easygoing Tom Lewis. When Burney was born in 1914, his father had raised no objection to naming him after his wife's first husband who had also been a good friend of his.

For that matter, Tom Lewis was in no position to object, having moved into the Burnett house when he married Burney's mother thereby depriving himself of any authority he might otherwise have had. Before that he had lived in the Pemberton house, never in his life, in fact, setting up an establishment of his own. Miss Bessie, at the time of his remarriage, elected to remain with her grandfather from whom she would eventually inherit all his property as his only heir.

"Basement window locked now, Miss Bessie?" Burney asked.

"Certainly is. And every other window in the house too. I'll put the chains on when you leave and I'll be just fine."

Her voice had lost momentum. She had talked herself out on the subject of the dead man in the cellar. "Make us all a drink before you go, Burney," she said.

On the way home Price said to her husband, "There really was a man, you know."

"Yes. Not a dead man, though. Like the police

said, he probably knocked himself out falling down the stairs and then got away through the window before they arrived."

"A sneak thief. Miss Bessie surprised him before he could steal anything. He didn't get in through the library window, though. Walked right in through the side door. Or found the basement door unbolted like it was the other day. Of course she wouldn't admit she had forgotten it."

"Far as I know, she never admitted she was wrong about anything in her life," said Burney.

Price laughed but when they got home called Miss Bessie to make sure she put the chains on the doors before she went to bed.

"I've already taken care of it," came the reply.

The spare key in the trellis didn't enter Miss Bessie's mind. She was too accustomed to its being there; couldn't even remember when she had last had occasion to use it.

Hunger forced Henry out of his motel bed at seven o'clock that night. He fortified himself with two drinks before he felt equal to getting dressed, moaning over his aches and pains.

Food helped a little but not enough for him to try to reach Krupusiak at home. That call could wait until tomorrow.

Henry felt better Thursday morning after a hot tub and treatment of his injuries. He could even get his eye open halfway.

He put on his other suit, carrying the one he had worn yesterday out to his car to be cleaned and mended at some cleaner's in Kingston. After breakfast he was ready to tackle Krupusiak.

The latter, who should have been off at one of his building projects, was waiting in his office for Henry's call.

"Well, Mr. Robin, sorry to hear my men exceeded their instructions again," he began.

"Your goons," Henry corrected him coldly. "Thugs, beating up a man my age. Not even a fair fight, two against one. And young enough to be my sons. Not that I would claim such creatures. They're lucky I didn't have them arrested for assault and battery."

Krupusiak refrained from pointing out that Henry was in no position to do anything of the sort.

"I'm sorry," he said again. "That's about all I can say, Mr. Robin. Except that you don't have to worry about them any more. I'm calling them off. We can go right ahead —"

"Oh no," Henry interrupted with no softening of his tone. "It's a new ball game now with new rules. There'll be no meeting at the Prince George. We'll meet at my bank in Kingston the one at the shopping center as your goons have probably told you. You hand over the money, I take it into one of the cubicles, count it and put it in my safe deposit box. Then, and only then, I turn the deed over to you."

"That's a hell of a way to do business," Krupusiak protested for form's sake. "How do I know you'll turn the deed over to me once you get the money?"

"Because I'm different from you, Mr. Krupusiak. Because I keep my word as a gentleman should."

The nerve of the blackmailing bastard calling himself a gentleman, thought Krupusiak with all the indignation of a self-made man who didn't have a gentlemanly bone in his whole body.

But he kept this feeling out of his voice as he went on protesting a little longer before he finally said, "Well, if that's the way it is, reckon I'll have to go along with it. When do you want me to meet you at the bank?"

Henry hesitated. "I'll have to think about it. I'm not sure yet."

Goddamn right you're not, Krupusiak reflected, certain now that the deed was still in Miss Bessie Lewis's house and that Fletcher didn't know just when he'd be able to lay hands on it.

"Let's see, tomorrow's Friday," Henry continued. "Maybe then. If not, the bank will be closed over the weekend and it will have to go till Monday. I'll call you and let you know."

"Monday suits me better," Krupusiak said wanting to give Breck and Elwood all the extra time possible to grab the deed ahead of Henry.

"I'm not interested in what suits you," Henry said sternly. "I told you I'm making the rules now and we'll meet at a time that suits me. I'll let you know when that is." He paused. "And by the way, I'm adding expenses from Monday on when I was ready and willing to hand the deed over to you. Fifty dollars a day will be about right."

"Jesus, you're really putting the screws on." For an angry moment Krupusiak reacted as if he intended to keep his end of the bargain. It would be a pleasure to kill the fat old windbag himself with his bare hands.

"Furthermore," Henry added, "this is your last chance to deal with me. If there's any more bad faith on your part, any more assaults on my person, in

180

fact, if I so much as lay eyes on those goons of yours again, the whole thing is off. The deed will then go to a certain person you'll never be able to settle with, who'll have you bankrupt, dragging you through the courts for years. Just bear that in mind, Mr. Krupusiak."

"Don't worry, no hitches this time." The dumb jerk really seemed to think Krupusiak had just been sitting this thing out, letting him call the turns, not even trying to find out for himself who the owner of the deed was. Give him a real jolt to say, "Oh you mean Miss Bessie Lewis, your ex-wife?"

He wouldn't, of course. It wasn't his style. He did business by getting the goods on his opponents while playing his own cards close to his vest.

"We'll see. I'll be in touch with you." Henry hung up.

He drove to Kingston, dropped his suit off at a cleaner's and then went on to Cranston Street to go through his usual routine.

No sign of the goons. (Henry, in his innocence was still looking for the Firebird.) Miss Bessie's car was in her driveway. Henry sighed. A gray day like this, threatening rain, she was probably going to stick close to home.

He bought the Washington *Post* at a newsstand and read it in his car. At noon he drove past Miss Bessie's again. Car still in the yard, no sign of the goons. The maid would be arriving soon. That would put an end to any hope of action before evening. Henry returned to his motel and took a nap.

He slept until after five o'clock. By the time he washed up, had a couple of drinks and dinner at the restaurant nearby it was close to seven.

It began to rain as he drove back to Kingston and was raining quite hard, bringing on early darkness by the time he arrived at 108.

The maid was leaving as he drove past. Lights on inside, Miss Bessie's car outside, none of it very hopeful.

Elwood kept well in back of him on the way to Kingston, certain of his destination. And parked the hired blue Ford he was driving far down the street when they reached it.

Breck was already patrolling the area on foot, beginning to get wet, retreating to Miss Bessie's garden when he spotted Henry who could at least keep dry in his car.

There was little activity on the street as time wore on. What there was, a party next door to Miss Bessie's, a big party that gave promise of lasting far into the night, didn't make any of the three watchers happy. Then there was the police cruiser that drove by the house twice. The second time, the driver got out and rang the bell to tell Miss Bessie he was going to take a look around and not to worry if she saw his flashlight out back.

Breck barely had time to get out into the alley before the officer appeared and even then wasn't safe as he came through the gate flashing his light around while Breck dived into the nearest shrubbery.

He went around the block in search of Elwood when the officer left. "We better not try anything tonight, El," he said. "Cops'll be back sure as hell. They was here last night three or four times too. By tomorrow night things ought to quiet down. There

182

won't be that party going on next door neither."

"But what if Fletcher tries to get in tonight anyways?"

"We'd have to follow him. But he won't."

"If he don't, should I tail him back to his motel?"

"No need. Mr. K. says he's stalling because that paper he's after is still in the house. We got to try to get it first. Tomorrow night, maybe."

Henry just sat in his car. At ten o'clock, when Miss Bessie's downstairs lights went out, he gave up for the night.

The newsstand he had stopped at that morning was still open. He bought a copy of the Kingston *Dispatch* which he hadn't read since his marriage ended. Might as well see if he still recognized anyone's name in it.

The officer who took over the patrol of Miss Bessie's area on the midnight shift drove by her house routinely once or twice during the night but didn't stop to check it. To hell with her, he thought, writing letters to the paper about how inefficient the police were.

They had tried to laugh it off at headquarters, calling her a nut but it rankled just the same. It was like when they were called pigs, they said it stood for patriotism, integrity, and guts, but nobody liked it any the better for that. From tonight on, Miss Bessie's would get less special attention. She had done herself no good with the Kingston police force. They were human, they had a right to have feelings, too, didn't they?

Henry read Miss Bessie's letter over a nightcap in his room. He shook his head remembering how she had embarrassed him when their marriage and his real estate and insurance business were both new, writing a letter to the *Dispatch* complaining that the city's insurance business wasn't being distributed fairly among the local agents.

She was still at it.

"Luckiest thing ever happened to me was the day she threw me out of her house," he said. "It calls for another drink."

While he was making it he gave thought to his protracted absence from Lennox. Here it was Thursday already and he would probably have to stay over the weekend or even longer. Paul Stevens would be wondering why he hadn't heard from him when he was only supposed to be gone for two or three days. Mrs. Taine too.

Easier to call her than Paul who might ask inconvenient questions. Late, of course, past ten-thirty, but still—

Mrs. Taine answered promptly, alertly, not awakened from sleep. "Oh, Mr. Fletcher. I've been expecting you back before this. So has Mr. Stevens. He called me this morning wanting to know if I'd heard from you."

"Unforeseen complications, dear lady. You know how they have a way of cropping up in business deals."

"Indeed I do. I well remember how after Edward died—"

"As I was saying about these complications—they may keep me here a few days longer, Mrs. Taine, which leads to asking a favor of you, if you don't mind."

"No indeed. What is it?"

"I tried to reach Paul Stevens tonight but couldn't. Would you mind calling him for me in the morning and explaining what the situation is? I have an early appointment that will keep me from calling him myself."

"Certainly, Mr. Fletcher. No trouble at all. But where shall I tell him he can get in touch with you if he needs to?"

"No way he can, I'm afraid, the way I'm moving around from here to there."

"But—"

"Don't worry about it, dear lady. Thank you very much. See you soon." Henry turned a deaf ear to another protest she started to make and hung up.

A difficult conversation handled well, he thought, but a bit trying just the same. He needed a drink to settle him down after it.

As it turned out, he needed two more before he went to bed.

## 21

Henry woke up Friday to a warm sunny day. As he drove to Kingston the air coming in his open window was fragrant with the scent of flowering trees and shrubs everywhere in bloom.

He wasn't nearly as stiff and sore as yesterday and could get his eye open most of the way, although it was still black and blue. In fact, his general feeling was that this was a day to accomplish things such as regaining possession of a certain deed in a certain house.

Breck and Elwood were sitting in their second rental car, the blue Ford. There were tourists about in considerable numbers, sauntering through the old section of the city admiring the elegant houses and gardens. Their activity made good cover in the whole area that included Cranston Street.

Henry parked his car some distance away and strolled among the tourists. No sign of the goons — who were down on the floor of the Ford when he went past on the other side of the street — he noted with satisfaction. Maybe, for once, Krupusiak had been as good as his word and called them off.

Maybe he would be able to just nip into the house this morning, grab the deed, call Krupusiak and have his money in his safe deposit box before closing time. He might just make it with the bank staying open until seven-thirty Friday evenings.

But he was not able to nip right into Miss Bessie's house when he reached it. There was a damn Plymouth in the driveway and there was Miss Bessie herself out front in her scrofulous garden outfit supervising the colored man cutting the grass.

Back and forth at discreet intervals during the morning. Car, Miss Bessie still there. God, was the woman glued to her house?

Then the maid arrived. Probably, though, hopeful thought, she didn't come weekends. If he had no chance to get in today, he should have a better chance tomorrow.

But today wasn't over yet.

Henry picked up his suit at the cleaner's and then had lunch. The expense of eating out three times a day was really piling up, he thought ruefully. To say nothing of his motel room and so on.

None of it would matter, of course, once he had his money.

He would have earned it. The goons beating him up, the risks he had taken, to say nothing of the deadly tedium of keeping watch on the house. He had never realized before how hard such work must be on detectives. Stakeouts, they called them, didn't they?

At quarter of six that evening as Henry strolled up Cranston Street—still tourists about, he was pleased to note—a middle-aged couple was turning in at Miss Bessie's. He didn't recognize Burney, his former brother-in-law, could hardly have been expected to, Burney having been an adolescent attending Fork Union Military Academy in his time. Price looked vaguely familiar from the glimpse he had had of her in the garden the other day.

Miss Bessie, no longer wearing her gardening outfit but quite dressed up for her, was outside to greet them.

"Lovely day," she cried. "Come out back and see how nice my garden looks. We'll have our drinks out there. Iris is down in the basement now getting out the lawn chairs."

The couple said something Henry didn't catch. The next moment, as he went past the house, the three disappeared around in back of it.

A few feet on he stopped short. Miss Bessie had said Iris was down in the basement getting out the lawn chairs. In other words, there was no one in the house just then, the door unlocked—

Henry turned back. It was a chance that might not come again.

Strike while the iron is hot, he told himself and walked boldly up to the side door prepared to ask directions to one street or another if anyone appeared.

No one did. He could hear voices, Miss Bessie's overriding the others', the scrape of furniture on brick. A quick glance around as he reached the door, heart beating faster, hand turning the doorknob.

A moment later he was inside, tiptoeing his way to the front hall and up the stairs. He had pulled it off. No one had seen him, he was safely inside, no need to sneak around after dark trying to get in.

He was mistaken, however, about not being seen. Breck, in the Dart now, parked across the way farther down the street, had watched Henry getting into the house from behind the newspaper he was pretending to read.

He admired the sheer nerve of it. He hadn't thought the old guy had it in him.

Iris came up from the basement while Henry stood looking around the upstairs hall considering his next move. He retreated a few steps as the knocker sounded on the front door and Iris went to answer it.

Fletcher had got inside just in time, Breck noted, burrowing deeper into his newspaper as the front door opened to the new arrivals.

" 'Evenin'," said Iris to the Lancasters. "Miss Bessie's out back with Miss Price and Mr. Burney."

Burney. The name clicked with Henry straining his ears from upstairs. Good God, the middle-aged man he'd seen was Miss Bessie's half brother who'd been just a kid in his time. How could the years have slipped by so fast?

"Well, now we're in, Joan, we might as well go out back by the side door," a male voice said.

Joan. Hadn't there been a young cousin, Joan somebody, who had just got engaged in his time?

Henry felt hopeful about the new arrivals as their steps faded below and the side door closed after them. Maybe Miss Bessie had just invited them over for drinks and they were all going out to dinner later. If this happened, the maid wouldn't stay long after their departure and there would be no problem about getting the deed back and then leaving at his leisure.

With the bank closed, there would, of course, be the problem of keeping it safe over the weekend. Not that he was too much worried about it; Krupusiak, it seemed, really had called off his goons. Talking turkey to him yesterday had done some good after all.

Even so, it might be wiser to move into the Prince George, Henry reflected. He could then put the deed in the hotel safe and feel completely easy in his mind until the bank opened Monday.

Never mind that now. He could hear Iris's footsteps moving back and forth below and he had better find a safe place to hide before she took it into her head to come upstairs for something.

Henry sat down on a chair in the hall to take off his shoes, not trusting himself, with all the sore spots he still had, to bend over standing up. He tied the laces together and tiptoed from room to room in his stocking feet.

At first it seemed a Tweedledee-Tweedledum choice between two back bedrooms that looked as if they never saw much use. But one had a closet he could take refuge in if the need arose whereas the other had only a big old wardrobe; and so he settled for the room with a closet.

From the rear window he looked out from behind the curtain into the garden. Five people sitting around on the lawn, Miss Bessie, Burney beside the woman who must be his wife, the couple Iris had admitted later. Not a real party, it seemed. Just the five of them having drinks with a tray that held the makings of refills on a table.

Soon now, perhaps, they'd all leave to go out to dinner. Henry held to this hopeful view until the clink of china and silver robbed him of it as Iris moved back and forth between dining room and kitchen putting the finishing touches to the table.

Miss Bessie's guests were staying for dinner.

How late would they stay? And how long, after they left, would it take Miss Bessie to get to bed and fall into a sound sleep?

Hours, he thought dismally, perennial optimism failing him. Three, four, five hours . . .

Tantalizing smells drifted up from the kitchen. Rib roast, maybe?

He became aware of the first pangs of hunger. Here he was, faced once again with the prospect of having to go without his dinner. His whole schedule had been upset since this affair began. All Krupusiak's fault too. If he had acted in good faith, as Henry had himself, it would all have been settled and done with days ago. It wasn't right to have it go on like this. It was bad for Henry's health. At his age, a man needed his meals at regular hours.

He couldn't even risk the comfort of his pipe.

And once again, the matter of his bladder was

bound to come up. Last time he had been trapped in this house, he'd at least had fairly safe access to the sink in the basement.

There were sinks up here, of course. Maybe, after they were all seated at the dinner table with Iris serving them . . .

When Elwood came up the street half an hour later Breck told him about the daring move Henry had made.

"Dead certain now that deed's still in the house," Breck said. "The liberry. Fletcher's going to wait till the company's left and the old bat's gone to bed. Then he'll go get it."

An eager look came to Elwood's moonlike face. "So all we got to do is wait outside and nail him when he comes out?"

Breck shook his head. "Dunno, El. Be late, be dark — what if we missed him again? I wouldn't want to be the one to tell Mr. K."

"Well, what should we do, Breck?"

"Maybe I should call Mr. K. and see what he thinks. Look, El, you go get your car and drive around the block. When you get to the corner I'll pull out and you take over my parking space here."

A worried frown chased eagerness from Elwood's face. "What should I do if Fletcher comes out before you get back, Breck? I mean, what if he gets the chance to grab the paper while them people are still out back? You want I should follow him?"

"Yes. But it won't happen. He won't push his luck that far. It's not just the people out back. The nigger maid's around somewheres too. So get going, El. I want to make that call to Mr. K., case he has plans for tonight."

"He won't. He said he was sticking close to home or his office until this thing gets settled."

"I said get going, din't I, El?"

Krupusiak was home and irritated by Breck's call.

"Chrissake, what do I hire you for, Breck? I got no crystal ball to tell me how things are going to work out up there tonight. You got to use what few brains you got yourself. All I can say is, once it's dark close in on the house, be ready to grab Fletcher the minute he comes out or get inside yourselves if it looks like a better deal. Surely to God, the two of you can handle Fletcher and that one old woman, can't you?"

"What if some cop starts poking around, though, like they been doing?"

"You seen much of them today?"

"Well, not really . . ."

"Goes to show. Excitement over the other day is over. Besides, cop comes around, you got feet to pick up and run with."

"Well, I just wondered what way you thought was best, Mr. K."

"No, that's not it, Breck." Krupusiak's tone hardened. "You want me to call the shots so you don't have to take the blame if something goes wrong. You're slipping, Breck, you and Elwood. You're letting old Fletcher get on your nerves. Looks like I need to get myself a couple of new boys."

"No, no, nothing like that, Mr. K. We'll make out

all right."

"You better, Breck, you better."

Krupusiak hung up.

Breck wiped sweat off his face as he hung up too. Mr. K. was a hard man, an unreasonable man sometimes.

He was the only man Breck had ever been afraid of.

## 22

A police car drove by Miss Bessie's around eight that night. All the lighted windows meant company, the driver thought.

Iris didn't finish clearing away dinner until after eight-thirty. Miss Bessie, tight with money, might pay her for her extra time or not. She might just remind her that two of three times a month when she was going out to dinner, Iris got off an hour or so early. Iris wouldn't know what her decision was until next Wednesday when she received her weekly pay check.

It was dark by that time. Breck and Elwood moved close to the house right after Iris left, Elwood from the alley, Breck from the street.

Elwood kept an eye on the gate ready for a quick escape if a cop came into the yard. Breck took up position behind Miss Bessie's car. He could run faster than Elwood, would be treading on his heels at the gate in back if a cruiser stopped out in front.

Only the front door was left uncovered. But

Fletcher would hardly come out that way, not with the old bat's bedroom right up overhead and her light on late.

Breck and Elwood were as familiar now with Miss Bessie's bedtime habits as Henry.

An hour went by. No one appeared, nothing happened.

At least it wasn't raining like last night, Breck consoled himself.

But where the hell was Fletcher hiding all this time?

At that particular moment Henry was trying to calculate how many hours ago he had last had nourishment, taken in the form of a sandwich and a bottle of beer. Had he had it one o'clock or one-thirty? It was now nine-thirty on the dot, going by the grandfather clock downstairs. So he had gone either seven and a half or eight full hours without a mouthful of food. No wonder he was prey to this terrible gnawing hunger. It was a well-known fact that the stomach required sustenance every five or six hours. His was rumbling away constantly. Gas, of course, the way he always got it if he missed his mealtimes.

To make it worse, there had been all those tempting smells from below, the sounds of dinner in progress. A good dinner, certainly. Miss Bessie, to give her credit, had always set a good table. Inviting him to meals had been one of the few lures at her disposal when they first became acquainted.

Henry sighed, smothered a belch and patted his paunch commiseratingly. God only knew when he would eat himself tonight.

But at least the group had moved across the hall to the living room quite some time ago, Miss Bessie then asking everyone what they would have, from which Henry deduced that liqueurs were being served.

Surely it wouldn't be much longer until they all left.

There had been no sudden alarms, no retreats to the closet during his sojourn in the back bedroom. There had been only the tedium of his long wait. No one, at any time, had come upstairs.

There'd be no tedium later on, though, when Miss Bessie came up to bed. There would be the suspense of waiting for her to settle down for the night and then the ticklish business of tiptoeing downstairs once she was asleep.

Henry hoped she still snored. The three years of their marriage she had snored every night but indignantly denied the whole time that she ever snored at all.

At last, not long after nine-thirty, sounds of departure came from downstairs, the group moving out into the hall thanking Miss Bessie for a delicious dinner and a very pleasant evening.

"Someday I'm going to steal Iris from you," one of the women said.

"Don't you even dare think of it, Joan," Miss Bessie exclaimed. "Best you can do is wait till I'm dead and gone."

"What good will that do me, Miss Bessie? You'll outlive us all."

"I might at that," Miss Bessie returned complacently.

Sounds of the front door opening and last good

nights. Then, from the porch, one of the women said, "Be sure you lock up good now, Miss Bessie."

"Indeed I will."

Sounds of the front door closing and the chain being fastened.

Oh, damn it all, thought Henry, I'll have no way to fasten the chain on the side door after me when I leave. She'll be raising hell in the morning about someone getting into the house again.

But what did it matter to him once he was out of there with the deed in his pocket? She could put a barbed-wire fence around her house after that for all he cared.

He slipped out of the bedroom to listen to her moving around. The tinkle of glassware told him she was gathering up the liqueur glasses, talking loudly to herself about overflowing ash trays and what a dirty, unhealthy habit smoking was, meanwhile clattering back and forth to the kitchen—what a noisy woman she had always been—as she tidied up after her guests.

She made two or three trips. Then the phone rang. Henry, leaning over the railing, heard her pick up and say, "Oh, it's you, Price . . . No, not yet. Just puttering around for a few minutes and then I'll lock up and be off to bed . . . Well, I'm glad you did. I certainly enjoyed having you-all . . . Oh, by the way, I forgot to ask you while you were here . . ."

Miss Bessie was off. She should be good for at least five to ten minutes.

This might be his best chance of all. Strike while the iron is hot. It had worked earlier, he reminded himself, so why not now?

He hurried back into the bedroom, picked up his shoes, still tied by their laces, and hung them around his neck.

He took his time, listening to Miss Bessie from the head of the stairs before he started down them, putting one foot quietly after the other. It didn't seem likely that she could hear anything above the sound of her own voice, but still he took his time having no reason to think her ears weren't as sharp as they used to be.

Three more steps to go, then through the hall into the library, whisk the deed out of its hiding place, slip behind the door or, if the phone conversation gave promise of continuing indefinitely, out and away he'd go by the front door. Let her find the chain off, let her carry on about it, what cared he once he was off the premises?

Henry felt almost giddy with delight over the hardihood he was displaying, the cool disregard of risks. Why, an experienced housebreaker, someone he could presume to be no more than half his age, wouldn't dare follow in his footsteps tonight.

Miss Bessie was still talking as he slipped into the library saying under his breath, "Third shelf from the top, third volume from the left . . ."

One lamp was burning. It furnished all the light he needed as he crossed the room and reached up to the third shelf from the top.

But he had reckoned without Price who had no intention of being tied up on the phone at that hour of the night. He froze suddenly, the third volume from the left in his hand as he heard Miss Bessie say, "Well, all right, if Burney's calling you, I'll tell you the rest tomorrow. Good night."

The click of the receiver restored Henry's power of movement. He reached into the opening, grabbed the deed and pushed the volume back in place.

Three long stocking-footed strides carried him across the room as the kitchen light went off and Miss Bessie came out into the passageway.

Henry edged in behind the door, the deed still in his hand for fear that the brittle old paper might make a crackling sound if he put it into a pocket.

Miss Bessie started to turn toward the side door to fasten the chain but was distracted by noticing that a mirror directly ahead of her in the hall hung crooked. It was near the library door. Henry held his breath as she advanced to straighten it.

Outside the house Breck had got more and more worried since the two couples had left. What if Fletcher had somehow managed to sneak out a window or even out the front door while he himself waited out back with Elwood? How would he ever explain that to Mr. K.?

He wouldn't have a chance to. Mr. K. would fire them both so fast they wouldn't know what happened to them. He'd do worse, maybe. He'd fix it so they'd never get another job anywhere in the whole state of Virginia.

Fletcher had given them the slip twice already. Who knew what had become of the old bastard now, after hiding in the house all these hours?

Breck moved out from behind Miss Bessie's car.

The street was quieting down for the night. Footfalls a block away echoed in the silence.

God, even if they nailed Fletcher coming out of the house, how could they be sure they could silence him before he had a chance to yell and rouse the whole neighborhood?

Breck fingered his gun. Not with any thought of shooting Henry right there on Cranston Street but with the hope that he could shove it into his ribs fast enough to keep him quiet.

If things worked out that way.

Maybe he should have let El carry his gun, too, instead of leaving it back at the motel. But El got excited too quick. It had seemed safer not to let him carry it tonight.

Breck leaned against the car and heaved a sigh, burdened down as he was with the weight of decision.

Miss Bessie didn't draw her shades at night. All he could see of her, though, was the top of her head bobbing around in the kitchen.

Breck crept over to the door and tried it gently. It was locked but the key was in place in the trellis.

What to do? Where the hell was Fletcher? God, he could be sneaking out the front door while the old bat was busy in the kitchen.

Breck moved quietly down to the end of the driveway to look. No one in sight in either direction. But what did that prove?

He went back to his observation post by the car. The old bat's head dropped out of sight. She seemed to have sat down.

When he could stand it no longer, Breck gave a low

whistle, his signal to Elwood, lurking near the gate, to join him.

"Dunno about this, El," he whispered. "Getting on my nerves, the way Fletcher don't show. Reckon we better go in."

"Now?" Elwood hissed. "All the lights on, we don't know where the old bag is. What if she runs out and starts yelling or something before we can shut her up?"

"She's somewheres in the kitchen. We wait till she goes in the other room."

They went over to the door, Breck reaching for the key and putting it in the lock. The kitchen was now out of his range of vision. He waved Elwood back. "Give me the high sign soon as she goes in the other room and we'll go in."

Soon thereafter, Elwood crept over and pointed to the kitchen window. The light had just gone out.

They were over the threshold, tiptoeing in a moment or two later. But Miss Bessie, straightening the hall mirror, saw their reflection in it and whirled around.

"Who are you?" she demanded. "What are you doing here?"

"It's all right, ma'am. Don't get excited. Just looking for someone."

"And who would you be looking for in my house?" Miss Bessie reddened with anger. "Bursting in like hoodlums in the middle of the night, not even the manners to ring the doorbell—what are you really after? There's no one here but me. You get out right now, this very minute."

She was not in the least intimidated by the big hulking pair. She eyed Breck belligerently in sudden recognition. "Why, you're the man who was hanging around my alley the other night. Up to no good, I reckon. If you don't get right out of here I'll call the police."

"No, ma'am, no police." Breck drew his gun. "Don't want no trouble, ma'am. Just you back up, go into that room behind you, the liberry, and do like I tell you."

"Why—" Miss Bessie sputtered, not able to believe her eyes as she took in the gun. "Why, the very idea—"

But she backed up slowly, still sputtering, face so red now that she looked ready to burst a blood vessel.

"El, take a good look around," Breck directed keeping his eyes and his gun fixed on Miss Bessie. "Upstairs, downstairs, closets, basement—pull the shades down, though, before you turn on any lights. Take a good look now, under the beds, everywhere."

"Sure thing, Breck." Elwood headed for the stairs.

"All right, ma'am," Breck said when he had Miss Bessie backed into the library. "Just take it easy. Sit down over there." He gestured to Grandfather Pemberton's chair. "Sit down and keep quiet and nothing will happen to you."

Miss Bessie could not, of course, keep quiet. She went on sputtering as she sat down. "Never heard of such a thing in all my born days . . . What's this outlandish story of looking for someone in my house? I told you there was no one here but me.

You're burglars, that's what you are, come to steal my beautiful things—"

Miss Bessie broke off squawking with fury as Breck, paying no attention to her, scanning the bookshelves and remembering what Krupusiak had said about hiding the deed behind old books no one ever looked at, advanced on Grandfather Pemberton's law books, reached up to the top shelf and began to pull them out one at a time, shaking the leaves and dropping them on the floor.

"How dare you!" Miss Bessie sprang to her feet, rushed over and grabbed Breck by the arm. "Let my grandfather's books alone. Oh, you vandal, you dreadful redneck! Stop it, hear?"

"Ma'am," Breck said in boredom and fended her off with a casual backhand that sent her sprawling against a chair.

She was up in a moment, swooping over to the fireplace to snatch up the poker. "Barbarian! Scoundrel!" She belabored him with wild flailing blows from which he ducked back, trying to get the poker away from her without being too rough about it since he hadn't quite shed his awe of her from the other night.

He tried to dodge behind the door to escape her but found the space already occupied.

He and Henry gaped at each other.

Breck was quick to recover. "My God, El," he bellowed, still fending Miss Bessie off with one hand. "Come down here. I just found Fletcher."

Heavy footsteps pounded overhead and down the stairs.

Miss Bessie's jaw flew open. "Fletcher?" she said, her hand holding the poker dropping to her side.

Breck nudged Henry out from behind the door with his gun.

"Well, Mr. Henry Fletcher, now you can save us the trouble of going through all them books."

"Henry Fletcher?" Miss Bessie stared beady-eyed at her ex-husband as he came out from behind the door.

## 23

The deed was still in Henry's hand when he was discovered. In a last desperate maneuver, hand behind his back, he let it drop to the floor. But when he pushed the door back closer to the wall to hide it, a corner of the envelope, a white triangle, conspicuous against the dark floorboards, slid out from underneath.

"What's up, Breck?" Elwood stopped short in the doorway, taking in the tableau, Miss Bessie with the poker now pointing straight ahead like a lance, Breck with his gun trained on Henry, ordering him to turn around and put his hands against the wall up over his head.

As Henry turned he saw the white triangle sticking out from under the door, tried to push it back with his foot and instead drew Breck's attention to it.

"There it is, El, there's the deed," Breck shouted. "Get it quick!"

Elwood hadn't seen it yet and looked confusedly at his colleague. "Where, Breck?"

"Holy Christ!" Breck lunged for it. Henry gave an anguished yelp and lunged too. They knocked heads, saw stars. Each got a grip on the envelope and tore it almost in half before Breck got it away.

A table crashed back against the wall. Elwood lumbered into the melee to help subdue Henry, still yelping and trying to get hold of the deed again. The blow Elwood aimed at him somehow caught Breck on the jaw instead and slammed his head back against the door. He dropped the gun. It skidded across the floor close to Miss Bessie.

She snatched it up and scurried back to the far wall with it.

"That's enough!" she shrieked. "I've got the gun and I'll shoot every single one of you if you don't stop this ruckus this minute."

Gun. The word penetrated, brought the thrashing figures to sudden immobility except for Breck who kept on shaking his head to clear it of the haze left by Elwood's heavy fist.

"Get up now," Miss Bessie commanded and, as they struggled to their feet, Henry clinging to the doorknob for support, "Henry, put that table back where it belongs. And if it's damaged, one of you will have to pay for it. No, stay right where you are." This, to Breck taking a tentative step forward. "One more move from you and I'll shoot. Within my rights, too, hoodlums breaking into my house, tearing it apart."

Breck drew his foot back. Her stance was resolute, shoebutton eyes snapping at them through rimless glasses.

Henry broke the silence. "You want me to put the table back now, Miss Bessie?" he inquired meekly.

"Yes. Straighten out the rug under it first."

Henry's pipe fell out of his pocket as he bent over the rug.

"So you still smoke that thing," said Miss Bessie. "Disgusting. Pick it up off my clean floor."

Henry picked it up, put it in his pocket, carried out the rest of his orders and took his place in the lineup again.

"Now, you there," she pointed to Breck. "Give that paper—deed, you said?—you were fighting over to Henry so he can give it to me."

As Breck hesitated, she aimed the gun at his midriff and said, "I'll count to five and if you haven't given it to Henry by that time I'll shoot. One—two—three—"

Breck, sullen in defeat, handed the torn deed to Henry.

"Put it on the mantel, Henry."

Henry put it there. Miss Bessie, not taking her eyes off them, moved crabwise from her corner to pick it up and slip it down the front of her dress.

"Now, Henry—"

"Miss Bessie, is it all right if I get my shoes—they're over there near the door—and sit down to put them on? My legs—I'm not a young man—"

"All right, you sit down in that chair right behind you, put your shoes on and tell me what you and your villainous friends are up to."

"Friends?" he groaned. "How can you call them that when you saw what they were doing to me?"

208

"No more than you deserved, no doubt, sneaking around in my house . . ." She narrowed her gaze on him. "White hair, that black eye of yours — why, I declare, you're the dead man who was in my basement the other day!"

"Miss Bessie . . ."

"It's all tied together in some kind of scheme, isn't it? This paper, this deed" — she tapped her bosom — "you-all have been fighting to get hold of?"

He nodded wretchedly sagging in his chair, her voice cracking like a whip over his head, a reminder that he never could stand up to her.

"It's worth a lot of money, Miss Bessie — that land at Haydon's Run — "

"Money? And you were trying to steal it from me? . . . No, don't either one of you make a move." She glared balefully at Breck and Elwood who had changed position uneasily. "Speak up, Henry. I'm waiting."

Hope flickered in Henry's good eye as he made a last attempt to salvage something from the wreckage. "You wouldn't have known a thing about it, Miss Bessie, except for me. Seems as if I should get something out of it . . ."

"The nerve of you, Henry Fletcher," Miss Bessie cried. "The bare-faced nerve, after trying to steal it all from me. If you'd come to me like an honest man in the beginning, I might have been willing to listen. Not now, though, not after you bring in these ruffians to threaten a helpless old woman — no indeed, Henry Fletcher, you'll not get one cent of the money out of me. The police will take care of you."

Moving crabwise again, she headed for the phone by Grandfather Pemberton's chair.

"The police? Oh, my God, Miss Bessie, you'll ruin me," Henry cried and got stiffly to his feet. "Prison would be the death of me at my age."

Miss Bessie gave him an unyielding look. "You should have thought of that before you got mixed up in this crooked business."

"I know, I know. But if you won't let me go for old times' sake, think of your own position. Think of the scandal, your former husband in prison, people talking, laughing at you—"

He had touched a responsive chord at last. Miss Bessie was silent pondering what he had said. Scandal. People talking, laughing at her. It wouldn't do.

"But what about this pair if I let you go?" she asked. "They won't keep your name out of it."

"Oh, but they will. They have to. Because they know if they mention me, I'll bring in Krupusiak, the Richmond developer who's in back of the whole thing. And Krupusiak wouldn't like being involved, would he, boys?"

Henry eyed them admonishingly but they didn't look at him at all. Their attention was fastened upon Miss Bessie and the gun she kept pointed at them steadily.

"The best thing they can do is let themselves be charged with burglary, breaking into your house to see what they could steal," Henry continued. "As long as they don't mention me and in that way keep Krupusiak out of it, he should be ready to hire the best possible lawyers for them."

Breck's eyes flickered. The message had reached him.

"Oh, I don't know . . ." Miss Bessie pondered some more, finally said, "Well, I guess you can leave, Henry. Go out the front door like an honest man would. But for heaven's sake"—her glance went to his unruly white hair standing on end—"comb your hair first and try to look respectable."

Henry combed his hair.

"Now look up the police emergency number and dial it for me before you go. I don't dare take my eye off these creatures long enough to do it myself."

"You want me to talk to the police, Miss Bessie?"

"Of course not. Just dial the number and put the receiver down. Keep your distance from me, though. I don't trust you one inch either."

Henry looked up the number, dialed it, laid the receiver on the table.

"Now get out," Miss Bessie snapped. "Get out quick and don't let me ever lay eyes on you again, Henry Fletcher."

In the brief glance they exchanged each knew that the other was remembering the last time she had said that.

"Police Department. Morgan," a voice echoed hollowly at the other end of the line. "Police Department. Morgan."

Miss Bessie picked up the receiver. "This is Miss Bessie Lewis at 108 Cranston Street," Henry heard her say as he raced to the front door. "Send someone right away. I just caught two burglars . . . Yes, two, I said. I got their gun away from them . . ."

Whatever else she said was lost on Henry as he closed the door after him and hurried off to his car. Or tried to hurry with vanished dreams dragging at his steps.

There would be no affluent retirement to Florida now; no trips here or there, no line of attractive widows vying for his attention.

He reached his car, got into it, drooped over the wheel.

Nowhere to go now but home to Lennox; to Mrs. Taine, poorer in pocket, poorer in hopes.

Still, it was tomorrow before he'd have to face all that. Meanwhile, maybe he'd feel better after he had his dinner. Maybe he could think of something else then. Like that widow Paul had mentioned last week who was thinking of selling what sounded like a fairly good house. Maybe he'd get a chance to meet her. Maybe she was an appealing sort of woman and had a little money too.

A more immediate problem was where he'd find a restaurant open in Kingston at this hour. He'd better get a move on if he wanted a decent meal. To say nothing of a couple of drinks first. He needed to pamper himself a bit. He'd had a hard day.

As Henry drove off he heard a police siren in the distance.

At least the goons would get their just deserts. He could have told them not to tangle with Miss Bessie. He had never meant to himself.

Miss Bessie ordered Breck and Elwood out into the hall ahead of her when the knocker sounded on the front door.

They could hardly look at each other for the shame they felt, two big men who prided themselves on their toughness, held at bay by this little old bat whose head came no higher than their shoulders.

But she was a sharp old bat, too, they told themselves. She handled that gun like she knew how to use it — or worse, didn't, but would use it anyway if they made a move out of line. A .38, too, that could blow a hole in a man before he could cover half the distance of nine or ten feet she was careful to keep between them.

But Jesus, Breck thought in desperation, what would Krupusiak say? And how would they ever hold up their heads again when it was spread all over the newspapers?

In that mood marching beside Elwood with the gun trained on their backs, Breck signaled with a gesture, a form of code he and Elwood had used in other situations.

"Open the door," said Miss Bessie.

As Breck opened it, Elwood sprang to the far side. It was now or never for them. Two cops strode over the threshold. Breck and Elwood were on top of them before they could draw their guns.

Elwood had no luck at all. His cop was a judo expert who flipped him over his shoulder to land in a heap in the diningroom doorway.

Breck fared better at first as he tangled with his, Miss Bessie hopping around on the fringes of the action, not daring to fire her gun. But while Elwood was getting up groggily on one knee, his cop sprang to the other's assistance. They soon had Breck pinned to the floor and handcuffed to Elwood.

But then as the cops were dragging the pair to their feet, Elwood struggled with one of them and shoved him back against a table. A huge top-heavy Victorian vase that had stood on it from time immemorial went flying through the air and crashed in pieces on the floor.

"Grandmother Coleman's vase," Miss Bessie cried. "Her beautiful vase! Irreplaceable and you've broken it to bits!"

She had never liked it. Ugly ornate white elephant was how she had always thought of it but now it had suddenly become a priceless possession.

She ran around gathering up the pieces, exclaiming over the cop's clumsiness.

"Seems as if you could come into a citizen's house and arrest a pair of burglars without destroying valuable property at the same time. The Police Department will have to do something about it, you may be sure of that."

"You got no right to call us burglars, ma'am," Elwood protested. "You know we ain't. You know that's not why—"

"Shut up, El," Breck snarled. "Shut up. Mr. K.—" Elwood shut up.

"What d'you mean, you're not burglars?" one of the cops asked.

"Nothing," said Breck. "We got nothing to say. We got a right to see a lawyer. He'll do our talking for us."

"Later," said one of the cops. "Right now we're taking you in and booking you on the charge of breaking and entering. That'll do for a start."

"We didn't break in," Elwood said. "We just walked in—"

"Shut up, El," said Breck.

"Armed assault," Miss Bessie said. "I'll bring charges. Burglars threatening me with a gun. This gun here." It was still in her hand.

"I'll take it, ma'am," said one of the cops.

"Evidence," said Miss Bessie. "One of them dropped it, I picked it up—"

"Just dropped it, Miss Bessie?"

Thin ice. "Well, happened they bumped into each other . . ."

No contradictions from Breck or Elwood. Instead, a temporary alliance with Miss Bessie, they three against the long nose of the law.

There was a lot more here than met the eye, the cops realized. But not their business to sort it out. Let Detective Pearson tackle that end of it.

Meanwhile, Breck and Elwood, handcuffed together, were removed from the premises, Miss Bessie trailing the cortege outside, reverting again to the matter of the broken vase. "Enormously valuable. Monetary and sentimental value both. And irreplaceable. What will the Police Department do about it?"

"Detective Pearson," the cops said firmly. "Talk to him about it, ma'am."

Breck and Elwood were hustled into the back seat of the cruiser and driven away.

Miss Bessie went back into the house, clucking to herself over the vase as she gathered up the rest of the pieces and put them all into a basket to show to the detective who would arrive soon to hear her story.

Get Price and Burney over to try it out on them before the detective arrived. It would present a few problems, keeping Henry out of it, but she could manage, she assured herself with the confidence born of handling many an awkward situation in her lifetime.

She hurried to the phone. Two burglars had got into her house, she said, and she had surprised them in the library.

Horrified exclamations from Price. They had just gone to bed but would be right over. as soon as they got dressed.

Well, that was making a start at least with no mention of Henry.

Henry, after all these years. He looked a sight with his fat belly, his jowls and pouches. He needed a haircut too.

Henry, a thief, trying to steal from her —

Steal what? What was all that business of the deed?

Miss Bessie reached down into her dress front and took it out.

The first time she read it she didn't quite grasp the implications of the restrictive clause. Then, as she read it again, she thought about drinks being served in motels at Haydon's Run, built on the very land Great-grandfather Sheffield had given to the church.

. . . *any spirituous beverage, liquor, beer, ale, wine . . .*

The restriction had been violated. The land reverted to her.

The light of battle shone in Miss Bessie's eye as she locked the deed away in Grandfather Pemberton's desk. She would call her lawyer first thing in the morning.

The doorbell rang. Either Price and Burney or the detective had arrived.

# 24

*Reader's Forum, Kingston Dispatch, May 16, 1971*

To the Editor:

Although the Kingston Police Department deserves criticism on many grounds, I recognize that on occasion, in the discharge of their duties, they have the right of access to the homes of private citizens; that sometimes, in fact, they are summoned to protect the lives and property of those whose taxes pay their salaries.

Recently, I was faced with such a situation myself. I called the police to remove from my premises two burglars who had threatened me with a gun. While I did not need assistance in disarming them, having already taken care of this myself, I summoned the police to take the burglars away and lock them up.

In a moment of what I will call excessive zeal rather than clumsiness, one of the two policemen who responded to my call broke an heirloom vase, one that I had long cherished as of great sentimental as well as financial value. It would not be stretching a point to describe the vase as a museum piece.

When I brought this matter to the attention of the proper authorities — for I felt that I should at least be recompensed for my monetary loss — I was told that the Police Department had no insurance or fund of any sort — none whatsoever! — that would take care of it.

I feel that I am not the first citizen to suffer from this total lack of concern for private property; but I also feel that it should not be allowed to go on unchallenged.

It is my intention, therefore, to bring suit against the Police Department in this matter. Perhaps City Council will then begin to reconsider its attitude toward the budget. On the one hand, it takes a niggling approach toward such essentials as adequate insurance coverage for the various departments of city government; on the other, it throws away with spendthrift zest the taxpayers' hard-earned money on such frills as planning commissions that come up with nothing of consequence. One-way streets are a glaring example of what we can expect from them.

BESSIE C. LEWIS
108 Cranston Street

# TALES OF TERROR AND POSSESSION

**MAMA** (1247, $3.50)
by Ruby Jean Jensen
Once upon a time there lived a sweet little dolly, but her one beaded glass eye gleamed with mischief and evil. If Dorrie could have read her dolly's thoughts, she would have run for her life — for her dear little dolly only had killing on her mind.

**JACK-IN-THE-BOX** (1892, $3.95)
by William W. Johnstone
Any other little girl would have cringed in horror at the sight of the clown with the insane eyes. But as Nora's wide eyes mirrored the grotesque wooden face her pink lips were curving into the same malicious smile.

**ROCKABYE BABY** (1470, $3.50)
by Stephen Gresham
Mr. Macready — such a nice old man — knew all about the children of Granite Heights: their names, houses, even the nights their parents were away. And when he put on his white nurse's uniform and smeared his lips with blood-red lipstick, they were happy to let him through the door — although they always stared a bit at his clear plastic gloves.

**TWICE BLESSED** (1766, $3.75)
by Patricia Wallace
Side by side, isolated from human contact, Kerri and Galen thrived. Soon their innocent eyes became twin mirrors of evil. And their souls became one — in their dark powers of destruction and death . . .

**HOME SWEET HOME** (1571, $3.50)
by Ruby Jean Jensen
Two weeks in the mountains would be the perfect vacation for a little boy. But Timmy didn't think so. The other children stared at him with a terror all their own, until Timmy realized there was no escaping the deadly welcome of . . . *Home Sweet Home.*

*Available wherever paperbacks are sold, or order direct from the Publisher. Send cover price plus 50¢ per copy for mailing and handling to Zebra Books, Dept. 2080, 475 Park Avenue South, New York, N.Y. 10016. Residents of New York, New Jersey and Pennsylvania must include sales tax. DO NOT SEND CASH.*

# MYSTERIES TO KEEP YOU GUESSING
## by John Dickson Carr

**CASTLE SKULL** (1974, $3.50)

The hand may be quicker than the eye, but ghost stories didn't hoodwink Henri Bencolin. A very real murderer was afoot in Castle Skull—a murderer who must be found before he strikes again.

**IT WALKS BY NIGHT** (1931, $3.50)

The police burst in and found the Duc's severed head staring at them from the center of the room. Both the doors had been guarded, yet the murderer had gone in and out *without having been seen*!

**THE EIGHT OF SWORDS** (1881, $3.50)

The evidence showed that while waiting to kill Mr. Depping, the murderer had calmly eaten his victim's dinner. But before famed crime-solver Dr. Gideon Fell could serve up the killer to Scotland Yard, there would be another course of murder.

**THE MAN WHO COULD NOT SHUDDER** (1703, $3.50)

Three guests at Martin Clarke's weekend party swore they saw the pistol lifted from the wall, levelled, and shot. *Yet no hand held it*. It couldn't have happened—but there was a dead body on the floor to prove that it had.

**THE PROBLEM OF THE WIRE CAGE** (1702, $3.50)

There was only one set of footsteps in the soft clay surface—and those footsteps belonged to the victim. It seemed impossible to prove that anyone had killed Frank Dorrance.

*Available wherever paperbacks are sold, or order direct from the Publisher. Send cover price plus 50¢ per copy for mailing and handling to Zebra Books, Dept. 2080, 475 Park Avenue South, New York, N.Y. 10016. Residents of New York, New Jersey and Pennsylvania must include sales tax. DO NOT SEND CASH.*

## THRILLERS & CHILLERS
### from Zebra Books

DADDY'S LITTLE GIRL                            (1606, $3.50)
by Daniel Ransom

Sweet, innocent Deirde was missing. But no one in the small quiet town of Burton wanted to find her. They had waited a long time for the perfect sacrifice. And now they had found it . . .

THE CHILDREN'S WARD                       (1585, $3.50)
by Patricia Wallace

Abigail felt a sense of terror form the moment she was admitted to the hospital. And as her eyes took on the glow of those possessed and her frail body strengthened with the powers of evil, little Abigail—so sweet, so pure, so innocent—was ready to wreak a bloody revenge in the sterile corridors of THE CHILDREN'S WARD.

SWEET DREAMS                                 (1553, $3.50)
by William W. Johnstone

Innocent ten-year-old Heather sensed the chill of darkness in her schoolmates' vacant stares, the evil festering in their hearts. But no one listened to Heather's terrified screams as it was her turn to feed the hungry spirit—with her very soul!

NIGHT STONE                                   (1843, $3.95)
by Rick Hautala

Their new house was a place of darkness and shadows, but with her secret doll, Beth was no longer afraid. For as she stared into the eyes of the wooden doll, she heard it call to her and felt the force of its evil power. And she knew it would tell her what she had to do . . .

## CATCH UP ON THE BEST IN CONTEMPORARY FICTION
## FROM ZEBRA BOOKS!

**LOVE AFFAIR**                                   **(2181, $4.50)**
by Syrell Rogovin Leahy
A poignant, supremely romantic story of an innocent young woman with a tragic past on her own in New York, and the seasoned newspaper reporter who vows to protect her from the harsh truths of the big city with his experience — and his love.

**ROOMMATES**                                       **(2156, $4.50)**
by Katherine Stone
No one could have prepared Carrie for the monumental changes she would face when she met her new circle of friends at Stanford University. For once their lives intertwined and became woven into the tapestry of the times, they would never be the same.

**MARITAL AFFAIRS**                           **(2033, $4.50)**
by Sharleen Cooper Cohen
Everything the golden couple Liza and Jason Greene touched was charmed — except their marriage. And when Jason's thirst for glory led him to infidelity, Liza struck back in the only way possible.

**RICH IS BEST**                                       **(1924, $4.50)**
by Julie Ellis
From Palm Springs to Paris, from Monte Carlo to New York City, wealthy and powerful Diane Carstairs plays a ruthless game, living a life on the edge between danger and decadence. But when caught in a battle for the unobtainable, she gambles with the only thing she owns that she cannot control — her heart.

**THE FLOWER GARDEN**                        **(1396, $3.95)**
by Margaret Pemberton
Born and bred in the opulent world of political high society, Nancy Leigh flees from her politician husband to the exotic island of Madeira. Irresistibly drawn to the arms of Ramon Sanford, the son of her father's deadliest enemy, Nancy is forced to make a dangerous choice between her family's honor and her heart's most fervent desire!

*Available wherever paperbacks are sold, or order direct from the Publisher. Send cover price plus 50¢ per copy for mailing and handling to Zebra Books, Dept. 2080, 475 Park Avenue South, New York, N.Y. 10016. Residents of New York, New Jersey and Pennsylvania must include sales tax. DO NOT SEND CASH.*